A HATFUL OF DREAMS

Sally Williams works in a milliner's salon, but her ambition is to own her own shop. When she delivers a hat to Lady Isabelle Lazenby, she becomes flustered by Lady Isabelle's handsome cousin, Charles Carey — but finds herself attracted to the footman, Harry. However, Charles' interest in Sally causes a rift in her friendship with Harry, who also seems to be close with Maggie, Lady Isabelle's maid. Will Sally achieve her ambition? And could there be a future for Sally and Harry?

ROBERTA GRIEVE

A HATFUL OF DREAMS

Complete and Unabridged

LINFORD
Leicester

First published in Great Britain in 2007

First Linford Edition
published 2007

British Library CIP Data

Grieve, Roberta
A hatful of dreams.—Large print ed.—
Linford romance library
1. Love stories
2. Large type books
I. Title
823.9'2 [F]

ISBN 978–1–84782–034–1

Published by
F. A. Thorpe (Publishing)
Anstey, Leicestershire

Set by Words & Graphics Ltd.
Anstey, Leicestershire
Printed and bound in Great Britain by
T. J. International Ltd., Padstow, Cornwall

This book is printed on acid-free paper

1

The door to the milliner's salon was ajar and Sally could hear Madame Chantal's voice murmuring an apology. She clutched the bundle of ribbons, waiting to hear the client's reply. She didn't have to strain very hard as Her Ladyship's voice rose in pitch, reaching a degree of hauteur matched only by that of the Duchess of Clanfield. But Lady Isabelle Lazenby was no real duchess, just a nobody who'd married well — so Madame said.

'And, why, pray, is it not finished? Did I not impress upon you that I simply must have it today?' The imperious tones vibrated in the air.

Sally stood by the door, trying to decide what to do. Her first impulse had been to storm in and berate their illustrious client. The hat was finished and wanted just a few finishing touches.

But poor Madame Chantal was barely recovered from a bout of influenza and her hands had been trembling too much for her to attempt the last few stitches. Surely Her Ladyship could make allowances for illness?

Earlier, Sally had tried to persuade her employer to let her sew on the ribbons and silk flowers.

'No, I can't allow it. Her Ladyship insists that no apprentice should work on her hats — you are well aware of that, Sally,' Madame had said. 'Just let me rest a little and I'll finish it off later.'

Sally sighed. She might have known that a lowly apprentice would not be allowed to touch it, however neat her stitches, however sure she was of her ability to design and make hats every bit as beautiful as those Madame created.

One day, she vowed, she would have her own salon — she would design such beautiful hats that all the ladies who paraded at Ascot and Goodwood would want them. She would be so successful that she would be turning clients away — including the obnoxious Lady Isabelle, who was still berating Madame Chantal.

She smiled ruefully and retreated to the workroom. Girls from poor families like hers seldom got the chance for an apprenticeship. They worked in the factories or went into service. It was only her widowed mother's hard work and determination that had seen her get this far. Still, it didn't hurt to dream — and dream was all she would do if she didn't work hard and finish her apprenticeship.

She put the ribbons on the work bench and gazed at her Ladyship's almost finished hat — a confection of rose and lilac silk, cunningly draped around the crown so that the colours shifted and blended in the changing light. It was lovely, even in its unfinished state. A spray of silk flowers in deeper shades of pink and mauve lay on the bench beside the hat stand.

Sally picked it up. She knew she

could finish the work in no time, if only Madame Chantal would allow it. But no stitches, however delicate, could match her employer's painstaking work. At least she would never admit it, Sally thought — never admit to her failing eyesight due to long hours working in bad light, or the fingers gnarled and misshapen with age. And she was still suffering the after effects of influenza.

Sally raised her eyes as she heard Lady Isabelle's loud voice. 'I insist on it being delivered — by noon at the latest.'

Her hackles rose. Didn't she care that Madame Chantal was ill? Without thinking, she barged into the salon, a protest on her lips.

Her Ladyship's head swivelled on her thin neck, eyebrows raised at the intrusion.

'My assistant, Miss Williams,' Madame said quickly.

Seeing her employer's warning glance, Sally forced herself to be polite. 'Would

Her Ladyship like some refreshment while she waits? The hat wants only a few more stitches. I have laid everything out in the workroom, Madame.'

Lady Isabelle stood up and beckoned imperiously to her maid, who stood, eyes downcast in a corner of the room. 'I am much too busy to wait. I do have other calls to make you know.'

Madame gabbled yet another apology, but Her Ladyship want on, 'If it is not delivered on time, I shall take my custom elsewhere — and I shall ensure that my friends and acquaintances do likewise.' She drew her gloves over her narrow fingers, picked up her bag and swept out of the salon, the maid scurrying behind.

At the door, the maid raised her eyes and smiled at Sally, covering her mouth with her hand as Lady Isabelle turned and glared. 'Remember — noon sharp and not a minute after.'

When they had gone, Madame Chantal sank back in the chair behind her desk, hands trembling, her breathing ragged.

She was very pale and beads of sweat gleamed on her forehead.

'Madame, are you all right? You should rest,' Sally said.

'How can I rest? You heard what she said. Oh, Sally, I shall be ruined.'

'I am sure your clients will remain loyal, despite Her Ladyship.' Sally tried to reassure her. 'After all, a hat by Madame Chantal . . . '

'Lady Isabelle Lazenby has a great deal of influence. She is constantly extolled a leader of fashion. If she goes to another milliner . . . ' Madame's voice faded into silence.

'She knows there's not another in town to match you, Madame. I'm sure it was just an empty threat.'

'You're wrong, Sally. She means what she says. And once she passes the word around . . . '

'She won't get the chance. We'll finish her hat and deliver it by noon if it's the last thing we do,' Sally declared. 'I'll take it round myself.'

Madame summoned a weak smile

and struggled out of her chair. 'I'd better get on with it then.' She took a step towards the door. 'Oh, dear. I feel quite giddy.'

Sally took her arm and helped her to sit down. 'You ought to be in bed, not trying to work. Why don't you let me finish it off?'

Madame Chantal pursed her lips. 'Oh, that would never do. You know how particular Lady Isabelle is.'

'If it's not delivered today, you'll lose her custom anyway.' Sally decided it was time to stand up for herself. 'Madame, forgive me, but you have told me my stitches are almost as fine as your own. Do you think Her Ladyship will know that I have done the work instead of you?'

'I'll know,' Madame said sharply. She clutched her hand to her chest and started to cough.

Alarmed, Sally ran to fetch a glass of water.

'Thank you,' Madame gasped when she was able to breath again. Her eyes were streaming and she held a shaking hand in front of her face. 'It seems I have no choice, Sally.'

'You won't regret it. I'll do the best work ever.' Sally's smile lit up her pale face and her blue eyes danced. It was the chance she'd been longing for.

She helped Madame into the work-room and settled her into a chair. The room at the back of the premises was half the size of the salon where Madame entertained the clients and discussed their requirements. A bench ran along one wall under a tiny window which looked out onto a brick wall. Even on the brightest days, little light entered and the gaslight burned for most of the day.

Sally pulled her stool up to the bench and studied the sketches Madame had made although she knew them off by heart. She took the hat off the stand and threaded a fine needle with lilac silk thread.

As Sally began the delicate task of attaching the silk ribbons, her fingers trembled nervously. She had to make sure that the stitches on the underside were as invisible as those which showed. It was hard to concentrate, knowing that Madame was watching, but as she became absorbed in the work she loved, she forgot her employer. Finally, she attached the little pink veil and with a satisfied sigh, fastened the last thread and reached for her scissors.

★   ★   ★

Sally's feet almost danced as she hurried through the narrow dusty streets clutching the hatbox. Madame had given her the money to take one of the new motor buses, but Sally still felt nervous riding on them. Besides, it wasn't very far and she was confident she would get to the elegant Georgian house in St. Martin's Square in plenty time.

Sally was elated with her success and the praise Madame had heaped upon her, and she'd introduced her to Lady

Lazenby as her assistant, not as an apprentice. At last she felt there was a chance for her to realise her dream. It had been a struggle for her widowed mother to find the money for an apprenticeship, but she'd wanted Sally to have the same chances as her older brother — no going in to service for her children.

George was now a qualified joiner and Sidney was a sergeant in the Army. Now, Sally thought, her mother had reason to be proud of her too. And if she ever achieved her dream she would be able to help her younger brothers and sisters to have their chances too.

She wasn't one of these suffragettes that were being talked about, wanting votes for women, but she couldn't help agreeing with them that it was time women had more of a say in their own lives. It shouldn't only be widows forced to earn a living who were allowed to run their own business, like Madame Chantal.

Sally knew what she wanted from life

and she also knew she was as good, if not better than Madame. Her head was always full of ideas for new designs. Although she was sorry for her employer, the illness had given Sally the opportunity to prove herself. Her apprenticeship was almost over and she would be able to call herself a milliner at last.

Who knows, in a few years she might set herself up in her own little business — and start calling herself *Madame Something or other?*

She smothered a giggle, recalling that Madame's real name was Doris Higgins. Not that there was anything wrong with 'Doris' as a name, but Sally had to agree that French-sounding names did better in the world of fashion.

By the time she reached the elegant town house in St. Martin's square she'd tried out several, Madame Estelle, Madame Babette. No, too much like music hall stars, or something worse.

Too late she realised she should have gone to the tradesman's entrance and she braced herself for a snooty reception from the butler.

She was about to hand the hatbox over and scuttle away before she got told off. But to her surprise, a footman in plum-coloured livery opened the door.

'Thank goodness you're here,' he said, almost dragging her inside before she had time to speak. 'Her Ladyship is in a terrible temper. The whole house is in an uproar.' He beckoned to a maid hovering in the background. 'Take her up quickly.'

Sally didn't want another confrontation with Lady Isabelle, but curiosity stilled her protests. She followed the girl up the wide curving staircase, taking in the gleaming crystal chandeliers, the gold brocade drapes at the long window on the landing. As she gazed round in awe she saw that the footman was till standing at the bottom of the stairs. He grinned, showing even white teeth and she couldn't help smiling back at him.

As they neared an open door, Sally

heard Her Ladyship's loud imperious voice. 'Where's that wretched girl got to? If she doesn't come soon I shall have to wear the blue and I had quite set my heart on the lilac.' There was a loud crash and a curse.

The maid tapped on the door, giving Sally a nervous smile.

'Come in, come in.'

'The hat girl is here, Ma'am.'

'And about time, too.'

The maid hurried away and Sally hesitated in the doorway, taking in the clothes strewn around the room, the broken vase in the corner. The girl who had accompanied Lady Isabelle that morning was holding up a gown of pale blue silk and, as Sally stepped into the room, Her Ladyship snatched it away and threw it on the floor.

'Well, bring it here, girl,' Lady Isabelle snapped. Behind her, the maid started to clear up the broken glass and Her Ladyship whirled round. 'Leave it. Fetch the lilac gown — now.'

'Yes m'lady'. The maid bobbed a

curtsey and went through to the adjoining room, pulling a face at Sally behind her employer's back.

Sally put the box on the dressing table and lifted the lid. How could Lady Isabelle fail to be impressed? The hat was beautiful — the best work that Madame, and she, had ever done.

Lady Isabelle sat at the dressing table, snapping her fingers impatiently. Sally took the hat from its box, smiling at her Ladyship's quick intake of breath. She hoped it was a gasp of pleasure.

She reached out a hand to adjust the ribbon at the back and Lady Isabelle knocked her hand away. 'My maid will do that,' she snapped, raising her voice. 'Maggie, here girl. Stop wasting time.'

Maggie came back into the room, a lilac silk dress, its bodice decorated with embroidered rosebuds, draped over her arm. The hat would complement the gown perfectly, Sally thought, although whether the outfit would compliment Her Ladyship was another matter.

Up close she had noticed a few grey threads in the blonde hair, lines of discontent around the eyes and a mouth that had once been beautiful. She was older than Sally had first thought and the dress and hat were far too young for her.

She held her breath as Maggie placed the hat almost reverently on her mistress' head, careful not to disturb the elegant coiffeur. Expecting criticism, she could hardly contain her smiles when Lady Isabelle turned and said, 'It's perfect'.

'Thank you, your Ladyship,' she said. 'Madame Chantal will be delighted.' She backed away, wanting to be gone before the woman changed her mind.

'Wait. I have not dismissed you yet. Tell me, did you have a hand in this?'

Tempting as it was to boast that she had done most of the work, Sally answered diplomatically, 'I am just the apprentice, your Ladyship. I do what Madame tells me to.'

Lady Isabelle raised her eyebrows

and smiled thinly. 'No matter. You may tell Madame I shall not be withdrawing my custom — yet,' she said, waving a hand in dismissal.

Sally hurried along the corridor and down the elegant staircase, her feet clattering on the polished marble. No doubt she should have tried to find the back stairs and left by the servants' door. But she just wanted to be out of there.

She remembered the first maid's nervousness and Maggie's defiant grimaces and reflected how lucky she was to work for Madame. She wouldn't want to be in service at the beck and call of spoilt pampered women with nothing better to do with their time than pick on the people they thought beneath them.

As she reached the bottom of the stairs, she glanced across the wide marble-floored hall. There was no sign of the good-looking footman who had let her in and she couldn't help a flicker of disappointment. She looked round, willing him to reappear and trying to tell herself it was because the front door looked so huge and solid she doubted she would be able to open it by herself and she didn't know how to find the servants' entrance.

The hall remained silent and empty. Surely in a house this size there must be someone who could show her out. She started towards the green baize door at the back of the hall, gasping as another door to the right opened and a tall elegantly dressed man with black hair and a small moustache came out.

She tried to shrink back into the shadows but he spotted her and smiled. 'What have we here, eh? Where did you spring from, young lady?'

'I'm sorry, your Lordship, I was delivering a hat to Lady Isabelle and I can't find my way out,' she stammered.

He laughed, showing white even teeth. 'Bless me, I'm not his Lordship. No one's ever mistaken me for that stuffed shirt before.' He chuckled again.

'I'm Charles Carey, Isabelle's cousin. And you are?'

Sally blushed and stammered. 'S-Sally Williams — apprentice to Madame Chantal, the milliner.'

'Well, Miss Williams, as no servants seem to be about, I must open the door for you.'

'Thank you, Sir.' Sally followed him across the hall, their footsteps echoing on the marble tiles. As they reached the front door, the footman appeared from a small room almost hidden behind the wide staircase. He hurried towards them.

'I'm sorry, Sir. Allow me,' he said, ignoring Sally as he hastily unbarred the heavy door and held it open. 'May I tell her Ladyship whether you will be back for dinner?' he asked.

'Bless me, Harry, my lad. I'm not going out. I was merely helping the young lady — since none of the staff was available.'

Charles Carey gave an unpleasant chuckle and Sally felt sorry for the young footman. Why did these upper class people have to be so nasty to those they considered the lower orders?

'I'm sorry, Sir. I was helping Mr Wilson in the pantry,' the footman said. Although he was apologetic he did not sound obsequious and Sally admired his straightforward manner until he straightened his shoulders and assumed a stern expression. 'As for you, Miss. Don't you know the front stairs are not for the likes of you?'

Sally's sympathy evaporated straight away. Cheeky devil. Besides, how was she to know where the back stairs were?

Lady Isabelle's cousin had been watching the exchange with an amused smirk on his handsome face. 'Now, now, Harry, leave the poor girl alone. I don't see the harm in letting her leave the way she came. After all, his Lordship's not home and my cousin is so busy getting dolled up for her garden party, she'll never know.'

The footman held the door and Sally hurried through it, her eyes downcast, anxious to get away. As she reached the bottom step Charles Carey called out, 'It was a pleasure to meet you, Miss Williams. I hope it won't be too long before the pleasure is repeated.' His low chuckle followed her across the square.

Her cheeks were burning. How dare he speak in such a familiar way? And how did he know she'd come in by the front door? He must have been spying on her. As for that footman and his pompous manner. Who did he think he was?

By the time Sally got back to the salon she had calmed down a bit. But the encounter with the two men had strengthened her resolve to have her own business one day.

Still, Charles Carey was very good-looking, charming too, although there had been something disturbing in the way he had looked her up and down. However, it was the tall fair footman in his fine livery that had stayed in her mind.

2

A few weeks later Sally had arranged with her friend, Rose, to go and listen to the band in the park. Determined not to entangle herself in affairs of the heart until she had at least finished her apprenticeship, she had been working extra hard and now looked forward to being out in the fresh air after being shut up in the work room all week. Rose Parker, a round-faced, pretty girl with rosy cheeks and red lips to go with her name, was anticipating making eyes at one of the bandsmen.

On this Sunday in early May, the girls walked arm in arm, dressed in their Sunday best, parasols shading their faces from the sun. Sally had begged a few scraps of trimming from Madame to decorate hers and Rose's Sunday straw hats and they felt themselves a match for the fine ladies who paraded the park with their maids following decorously behind.

As they approached the bandstand, Rose clutched her friend's arm and whispered, 'He's here.'

'Stop flirting,' Sally said sternly. But she smiled, knowing her friend meant no harm. It was just a bit of fun on her day off after the days of drudgery in the biscuit factory.

The Boer War had ended a year ago, but patriotic fervour had not lessened and the Guards' band, sweating in their stiff red uniforms played rousing marches.

Rose continued to make eyes at the handsome trombone player and Sally could tell he was having a hard time concentrating on the music. When he looked up and smiled, Rose blushed.

Sally turned her face up to the sun, enjoying the warmth and the feel of the slight breeze on her skin. She wished she had had the confidence to suggest that Madame Chantal joined them on their walk. She still seemed very frail, although the cough had left her now, but Sally was sure it would do her good to get out in the fresh air.

Rose had noticed someone else now and she clutched Sally's arm excitedly. 'Over there, Sal. Look — I'm sure he's got his eye on you,' she said.

'Don't be silly. If anyone, he's looking at you.'

'No, he's waving. Trying to get your attention.

Reluctantly, Sally turned and saw a young man with fair hair pushing through the crowd. As he got nearer she recognised Harry, the footman she'd encountered at Lady Isabelle's house and she couldn't help a little flush of pleasure.

Sally introduced him to her friend and, as the music ended, they all began to stroll towards the lake, Rose trailing behind and casting longing glances over her shoulder at the bandsmen who were now packing up their instruments.

Harry grinned at Sally. 'Sorry about the way I spoke to you before,' he said.

'Her Ladyship has us all on edge, minding your p's and q's.'

'I don't envy you, working for her,' Sally said. 'Mr Carey seemed nice enough though.'

Harry gave a short laugh. 'Oh, he's nice enough when he wants to be, just like her Ladyship. All smiles when things go their way, but watch out if not.'

'I don't think I'd like to be in service,' Sally said.

'It's not so bad,' Harry said. 'Besides, Lord Lazenby pays our wages — a good man, fair to his staff and tenants. Trouble, is he's seldom in town. Spends most of his time on his estate in the country. And when he's away, her Ladyship entertains all sorts — including her dear cousin, Charles.' He smiled at her. 'Let's not waste this beautiful day talking about them. Tell me about yourself — do you like making hats?'

'I love it.' Her face lit up in a smile. 'Working with those lovely materials — it's like a fairytale world,' she said.

Harry nodded encouragingly and she quite forgot about Rose as they strolled along together. She found herself telling Harry about Madame Chantal and how lucky she was to be apprenticed to such a well-known creator of fashionable millinery. She told him about her own poor background too and her ambitions to have her own salon one day. Suddenly, she stopped talking and gave a little laugh. 'Oh, hark at me rattling on. You must be bored silly.'

'Not at all. It's a treat to meet a girl with something sensible to talk about. You're like me, Sally — ambitious. I won't always be a footman, you know, I've got plans too.

She was about to ask what they were when she heard someone calling. It was Maggie, Lady Lazenby's personal maid.

The girl hurried up to them and grabbed Harry's arm. 'There you are. I've been looking all over.'

'You remember Sally, don't you?' Harry said.

'Yes, the hat girl. How could I forget,

you put her Ladyship in a good mood for once. Nice to meet you again.'

Sally tried to hide her dismay at the interruption. The two seemed very friendly. But when Maggie started to talk about her employer, she was fascinated. The ways of the gentry were completely foreign to her and she wanted to know more. As if she'd read Sally's thoughts, Maggie gave a little laugh. 'At least you made a hit with one of them.'

Sally felt herself beginning to blush, remembering the way Charles Carey had looked at her in the hall of St. Martin's Square House. But she recovered quickly as she realised Maggie was talking about her Ladyship. 'I ought to thank you really. As you saw, she can be a real harridan, but after she saw the hat, she was so delighted, she was sweet as pie for the rest of the day. She's recommending Madame Chantal to all her friends now.'

'Madame will be so pleased,' Sally said, longing to tell the other girl that she was responsible for the success of the hat. But Madame had sworn her to secrecy, fearing her reputation if it became known how much she relied on her apprentice.

Sally was doing more of the fine work now as Madame had never really regained her health and her eyesight had deteriorated even more over the past few weeks. Not that the older woman would admit it and sometimes insisted on doing the finish even when her health wasn't up to it. She resented any interference and Sally often had to call on all her reserves of tact and patience.

Maggie smiled, clinging possessively to Harry's arm. 'Come on, we have to get back soon and I don't want to waste any more of my precious time off.'

Harry raised his straw boater and allowed himself to be led away. Before Sally could say goodbye, Rose came running up, her face flushed and eyes shining.

'His name's Thomas and he wants to

meet me again,' she said, referring to the trombone player. While Sally had been chatting to the Lazenby servants, Rose had been busy too.

By the time Sally had replied, Maggie and Harry had reached the park gates ahead of them. As they disappeared from view, she tried to tell herself it didn't matter that Harry was so obviously already courting. Besides, she had no ideas of romantic entanglements.

When they'd gone, Sally tried to concentrate on Rose's chatter, pleased that their frequent visits to the park had borne fruit for her friend. Rose had been smitten with the young bandsman since she'd first spotted him back in the spring. 'He said he's noticed me listening to the band every week. I told him I love music, especially band music.

Sally laughed and Rose playfully punched her arm. 'Well, it's true,' she giggled. 'Don't you think he's good-looking?' She smiled dreamily.

'Good looks aren't everything,' Sally told her. Charles Carey was handsome and his lazy grin had sent shivers up her spine. But although he was exciting, he wasn't the kind of man she would fall for. It was Harry, with his wide blue eyes and honest open smile that had stolen her heart.

It was no use trying to deceive herself. She'd known the minute she spotted him across the park that she'd been hoping to see him again. And their conversation had only reinforced her feeling that if she ever did consider a romantic entanglement it would be a man like Harry Jenkins.

But it was no use. He was walking out with Maggie. Besides, she had an apprenticeship to finish and a career to launch before she could allow herself to fall in love.

★   ★   ★

'It's a lovely day,' Sally said, moving her chair closer to the window to take advantage of the sliver of sunlight that entered the little backroom. For a change the day was bright enough to be able to work by natural light and Sally was enjoying the warmth on her bare arms as she worked on a summer hat for one of the clients brought to them on Lady Lazenby's recommendation.

'I hope it stays fine for your outing to the races, dear,' Madame Chantal said as she sorted through the silks.

'Oh, so do I, it would be awful if it rained. All that mud — not to mention spoiling all the ladies' hats.'

Madame laughed. 'They only go to show off their finery. I'm sure they really have no interest in the horses.'

'It's so kind of you to let me have the day off,' Sally said. A group of Rose's friends at the biscuit factory had hired a charabanc and had invited Sally to join them on the trip to Epsom Races. After all, she had a new hat too and she didn't want it spoilt either. She glanced across to the stand in the corner of the work room where her pride and joy sat in all its glory waiting for the big day.

Ever since she'd put the finishing touches to Lady Lazenby's lilac hat, Madame had gradually allowed Sally to take on more of the fine work and had even accepted some of her suggestions for new designs. Ever since that bout of flu in the spring she had been ailing, prone to dizzy spells and coughing fits that left her weak and trembling.

She was worried about the business too. Despite the new clients, things weren't going as well as they appeared on the surface. The landlord had recently increased the rent on the salon, despite the fact that he had not done any repairs and the building was starting to get rather dilapidated.

One top of that their supply of materials was running low. All the ladies wanted dyed ostrich feathers these days. They were so fashionable that they were becoming scarce with a resulting increase in the price. But there was no money to buy more. Although many of their clients were rich, they had no qualms about making the lower orders wait for payment and Lady Lazenby was among the worst offenders. Madame was reluctant to chase them up for fear of losing their custom altogether.

Sally was made of sterner stuff and had offered to write out invoices to send to all those with outstanding debts. But Madame refused to allow it. 'They all pay eventually,' she said.

It wasn't good enough, Sally thought indignantly. She sighed. Madame was an artist when it came to creating hats, but she had no business sense. if *she* was in charge things would be very different. She glanced across at her own hat, picturing herself parading round the visitors' enclosure at Epsom. Maybe they'd catch a glimpse of the new King and his Queen or the Prince of Wales.

Madame followed her glance. 'You'll look an absolute picture, my dear,' she said. 'A good advertisement for the salon. You certainly have an eye for design.'

Sally flushed with pride. It had been quite an achievement to create a hat out of the remnants and odd and ends that littered the workroom. She had even included a small curl of ostrich feather that had broken off when Madame's hands had started to shake while unpacking a consignment.

She cleared her throat and tentatively made her suggestion. 'I could use these snippets and off-cuts to make more hats, Madame,' she said.

'Well, I don't mind, so long as you pay me for the felt and you do it in your own time. Did you want to make a bonnet for your little sister, or maybe a hat for your friend to wear to the races?'

'That would be nice. But I was thinking we could sell them — perhaps to one of those big new department stores in the West End. That way, the bits of material you can't use won't be wasted.'

Sally held her breath as Madame pursed her lips in consideration. But her shoulders slumped as her employer shook her head.

'Oh no Sally, that wouldn't do at all. I have my reputation to think of. I design individual hats to order for the gentry. No, no. Times are hard at the moment, but it will pick up, you'll see.'

It was no use arguing once Madame had spoken. Although her apprenticeship had ended and she was now Madame's official assistant, Sally was still an employee and as such had to do what she was told. She smiled diplomatically and said, 'Perhaps you're right, Madame.'

3

Sally's younger brother and sisters were asleep, tucked up head to toe like sardines in the big bed in the front bedroom of the terraced house in Tanner's Lane. She smiled and closed the door, went downstairs to where her mother sat at the kitchen table, her red work-worn hands clasped in front of her.

'All settled?' Ada Williams asked.

'Fast asleep,' Sally said, going to the range and pushing the kettle over the flames. She sat down opposite her mother. 'Madame hasn't paid me this week. I know she will when she can, but I'm worried. She's going to lose the business if she's not careful.'

'But you'll be all right, Sally. You can get a job anywhere with your training.'

'I expect you're right, Mum. But I don't like to let Madame down. She's been so good to me.'

'That's all very well, love. But you can't work for nothing.' Ada sighed. 'We can manage for a while, but . . . '

'I don't expect you to manage. You hardly earn enough to keep us all with your washing and ironing.' Sally bit her knuckle, took a deep breath. 'There's always my savings,' she said in a rush.

'Oh, no. I won't have you breaking into that. You've worked hard all these years and you've gone without nice clothes and things like other girls your age so you could build up your nest egg. No, I won't let you . . .

'You have no say in it, Mum. The boys need new shoes. I noticed this evening that Jimmy's have gone right through and Ronnie's aren't much better. At least let me pay for those.'

Sally hated the idea of spending her precious savings, but she couldn't see her little brothers suffering. She felt a brief flash of resentment at George, her older brother who paid barely the minimum for his keep and never offered to help out with a bit extra when times were hard. As for Sid, gallivanting off round the world with his regiment, clothes and food all round and money to spend on drink and women.

Sometimes Sally wished she had been born a boy. But, she told herself, she'd still have felt duty bound to help her mother and the little ones even though she sometimes resented it.

With a sigh, she went to the dresser and took down the battered old biscuit tin from the top shelf. Her mother gasped when she saw how much there was. 'Sally I had no idea . . . '

'It's taken me seven years to save this much. Every penny I could spare. I don't care how long it takes — I *will* have my own salon one day . . . ' Sally took out two half crowns and pressed them into her mother's hand. After a brief hesitation she added a few more coins, ignoring Ada's protests.

'I'll put it back when Madame pays me,' she said. While she had the tin down, she counted the money, large and small coins accumulated over the long period of her apprenticeship when she had earned scarcely enough to pay her keep. At this rate she'd be as old as Madame Chantal before she could open her own salon.

*   *   *

Sally was at the salon early next morning, anxious to get on with the orders. She had to add the trimming on the yellow hat that the client was due to pick up later that day. She had completed the job and wrapped the hat in its tissue paper, placed it carefully in a hat box and still Madame had not put in an appearance.

Worried now, Sally went upstairs to the attic rooms which served as Madame's living quarters. There was no-one in the tiny kitchen-cum-living room and Sally hesitantly opened the door to the bedroom. The curtains were still drawn and there was a fusty smell in the air. She could scarcely make out the small hunched figure under the eiderdown.

As she approached the bed, Madame sat up, eyes wide and staring. 'Who's there?' she croaked.

'It's me — Sally. Are you all right?'

'Oh dear. I must have overslept.' Madame pushed at the covers and tried to swing her legs over the side of the bed. But she fell back with a groan.

Sally rushed forward and drew the eiderdown over the frail body. 'Stay there and rest. I'll fetch you a drink,' she said. She straightened the pillows and brushed the wispy grey hair back from the old woman's forehead.

In the kitchen she filled the kettle and put it on the gas ring. Then she poured a glass of cold water and took it in to her employer, supporting her shoulders as she drank.

Pushing her hand away, Madame said in a stronger voice, 'That's better. Now I'd better get downstairs and start work.'

'Not today,' Sally said firmly. 'Everything's under control downstairs. You must stay here and let me look after you.'

'What about the yellow hat for Miss Davenport?'

'All done and ready for collection.' To Sally's surprise, Madame did not protest and insist on inspecting the work. She must be feeling really ill.

She went through to the kitchen where the kettle had now boiled. She made a pot of tea and poured the remaining water into an enamel bowl, topping it up with cold from the tap. She found a towel and took and the bowl into the bedroom. After carefully sponging Madame's face, she helped her to tidy her hair and propped her up on the pillows.

'Now I'll fetch you a nice cup of tea and some breakfast. You'll feel better when you've eaten,' she said.

'Not hungry,' Madame said. 'But tea would be nice.'

It was a good job Madame wasn't

hungry, Sally thought as she rummaged in cupboards in the kitchen. There was hardly any food in the house and no milk for the tea either. She ran downstairs and out of the salon to the little shop on the corner of the street where she bought a loaf of bread and a tin of condensed milk.

She'd wait until the client had picked up her hat then lock the salon and go to the market near where she lived. A few vegetables and maybe a knuckle bone from the butcher would make a good nourishing broth that would soon set Madame on her feet again.

When she got back to the salon, Miss Davenport was just descending from the her carriage. Sally hastily put her purchases on the bottom stair and closed the door, turning to greet the client as she entered the salon.

She reached for the hat box on the shelf behind the counter. Would you like to try it on, Miss?' she asked, lifting the lid.

'Oh, it's beautiful,' Miss Davenport

breathed as Sally lifted it from its tissue wrapping. 'I shall wear it to Ascot and be the envy of all my friends.'

She removed the hat she was wearing, sat in front of the gilt mirror and allowed Sally to place the new hat on her head. 'Oh, yes, I like it,' she said looking round the room. 'Madame Chantal has excelled herself. Where is she?'

Sally hesitated. Should she say Madame was ill? Better not. She smiled. 'Madame had an appointment. She'll be back soon.'

'I'll speak to her next time then.' Miss Davenport took the hat off and patted her hair. By the time Sally had re-packed the yellow hat in its box, the young woman had replaced her own hat, drawn on her gloves and was ready to leave. Sally carried the box outside and handed it to the driver who stood ready to open the carriage door for his mistress.

No mention had been made of payment. It was considered vulgar to talk of money. Sally knew that it would be a long time before she and Madame were rewarded for their hard work. Sighing, she locked the door to the salon and went upstairs.

★　★　★

When the broth was simmering on the gas ring and Sally had tidied the kitchen, she went down to the salon to see what work needed doing. She got the order book out of the drawer in Madame's desk, feeling a slight pang of guilt as she did so. She had never been allowed a glimpse of the business side, although she had picked up quite a bit in her years at the salon.

If Madame were to be ill for long, Sally would need to keep things running. She was sure Madame would forgive her for prying into her desk.

She sat down and opened the book, suppressing a gasp as she realised there was only one order outstanding — for Lady Lazenby of all people. Her

Ladyship had stipulated ostrich feathers Sally knew they did not have in stock. What was she to do?

She reached into the drawer for another book which contained sketches for designs. Usually, the neatness of the drawings and the notes accompanying them matched the neatness of Madame's stitches. But Sally was appalled to see the words scrawled across the page — 'Blasted feathers'. No wonder Madame was ill with this playing on her mind.

Sally put the books away and went upstairs. She opened the bedroom door and saw that the tea was untouched on the bedside table. The old woman stirred and opened her eyes.

'Still here?' she mumbled. 'You should be downstairs. Miss Davenport will be here soon.'

'She's already been — and she said you have surpassed yourself.'

The ghost of a smile passed over Madame's face and she struggled to sit up, wheezing painfully. 'You should have called me to deal with her. Miss

Davenport is a very valuable client. She has more influence in the fashion world than even Lady Lazenby.'

Sally was a little hurt that her employer was not more grateful for her help that morning as she helped her to sit up. 'I've made you some broth,' she said. 'Maybe I'll let you get up when you've had it.'

But after a few spoonfuls, Madame sank back onto the pillows exhausted. Sally took the bowl away and tidied the kitchen, a worried frown creasing her pretty face. It was obvious her employer would be out of action for some time. And with no money to buy materials, would she even have a business left when she finally recovered?

There was only one way out of the dilemma as far as Sally could see. She would have to lend Madame her savings — that's if the proud old woman would accept the offer.

Well, she wouldn't tell her — not yet.

As the sick woman slept the rest of the day away, Sally got out the books and made an inventory of all the materials and trimmings in the work-room. She made a list of outstanding accounts and resolved that, no matter what Madame said, she would send out invoices and reminders to all of them. She would also write to their suppliers and explain that Madame was sick. Maybe they would agree to supply goods against further orders.

By the time she had finished, twilight was darkening the corners of the salon. Sally lit the gas and went upstairs again. She fed Madame some more broth and settled her comfortably before reluctantly leaving her alone.

Sally did not tell her family about Madame's illness and if Ada noticed her delving into the tin on the dresser shelf more frequently, she did not comment. It was Sally's own money after all.

She had sent off the invoices and letters, written out in her best copper-plate handwriting. It was best to get it done and tell Madame about it when she was feeling stronger, she thought. If the business was back on its feet she could hardly be too annoyed.

The broth seemed to be doing the trick and by the end of the week Madame was able to get out of bed for half-an-hour. She wanted to go downstairs and see what was going on in the workroom, but her legs shook as she took a few steps across the room.

'I haven't thanked you for taking care of me, dear,' Madame said. 'But you shouldn't be doing this you know.'

'It's the least I can do. I'm glad to help out,' Sally said.

'But I can't pay you, Sally. You must know there was only one order and Lady Lazenby will be most unhappy when she calls to collect her hat and it is not ready.

Sally started to explain that she had already made a start on her Ladyship's hat, but Madame Chantal shook her head. 'I fear I shall be bankrupt, my dear. You should be out looking for another job. I shall give you an excellent reference. Any of the West End salons will be glad to have you . . . '

'We won't talk about it now. Wait until you're a bit stronger.' Sally wanted to be sure that the business was starting to recover before raising Madame's hopes. She had not really been surprised when few of their clients had responded to the letter she had sent. But two of the suppliers had delivered goods after Sally had paid part of the outstanding bills with her own money.

At this moment two ostrich feathers, dyed to a vivid kingfisher blue were waiting to be attached to Lady Lazenby's hat.

4

Sally had been so taken up with work and caring for Madame Chantal that she had quite forgotten the planned trip to the Epsom Derby. When Rose called the evening before the outing, excitedly talking about what they would wear, her face fell.

'I can't go, Rose,' she said.

'But your boss gave you the day off. It's all planned,' she protested. 'It's not fair. Is the old devil making you work after all?'

Sally explained that Madame was ill and that she could not leave her alone all day. 'She's slowly getting better, but I'm still worried about her.'

Rose pouted. 'I was so looking forward to it. It won't be the same without you. Isn't there someone else who could sit with her?'

Sally hadn't thought of that and her

face brightened. Her little sister, Jenny, was quite sensible enough to sit with the old lady. 'I'll ask Mum if she can spare Jenny for a few hours. After all, I have been working hard. I deserve a day off.'

'Of course you do. The old biddy will just have to put up with it.' Rose did not have much time for bosses.

Sally slapped her friend's arm. 'Don't call her that. She's very demanding when it comes to the standard of work. But she's a nice old thing and she treats me well so the least I can do is help her out now. Besides, if I don't keep the business ticking over I might not have a job for long.'

'You can easily get another job,' Rose declared airily.

Sally did not reply. She had once confided in Rose that she longed to have her own millinery and her friend had looked at her as if she was mad. 'You'll change your mind when you meet someone and get married,' she'd said.

Rose's ambitions were very different from her own. She didn't see the point of working for a boss when she could have her own home and a man to keep her. But Sally had seen the reality of that sort of thinking. Hadn't her own mother thought she was well-off with a husband in a good job and a cosy little house to bring up her children in — until Joe Williams had been killed in that dreadful accident at work.

Rose roused her from her thoughts. 'So you will come tomorrow?' she said.

'Yes, I will. I'll take Jenny round in the morning, explain what she has to do and make sure Madame's all right. Don't worry. I'll be at the factory by ten o'clock, but if I'm not there you'll have to go without me.'

The thought of earning a sixpence all to herself stilled any protests Jenny might have made about spending a sunny summer's day with an old lady and she willingly accompanied her older sister to the salon the following day.

She was only twelve but she was a sensible child, having had plenty of practise looking after young Ronnie and Jimmy while their mother was busy with the mountains of washing she took in.

Madame was looking a lot better today and Sally went off to join her friend with a lighter heart than she'd had for a long time. Although she still hadn't confessed to the changes she'd made in the salon, she was sure that when she was better and saw how the business was doing, Madame would see the sense of what she'd done — it was in her interests after all.

Sally turned the corner and saw Rose waving frantically from the top of the charabanc. As she climbed up and settled into the seat her friend had saved for her, she put all thoughts of millinery and Madame Chantal out of her mind and prepared to enjoy herself.

'You look lovely,' Rose said, admiring the hat Sally had spent so many hours designing and trimming. 'You could even get away with going into the Royal enclosure,' she giggled.

'Not quite, but I am pleased with it. I wish I'd had time to make one for you too,' Sally said.

'Never mind, I like this one,' Rose said. 'It's my lucky hat.' She was wearing the plain straw boat that Sally had trimmed for her and which she'd worn to the park that Sunday she had met Thomas.

'And how are things going with your trombone player?' Sally asked.

Rose blushed. 'I told you — his name's Thomas. He took me to the theatre last week and we're going out again tomorrow.' Her face fell. 'He couldn't get away today.'

'Never mind. We've got a lovely day to look forward to.'

Sally turned her face up to the welcome sunshine and allowed the tensions of the past couple of weeks to fall away. The charabanc left London behind and bowled through country roads towards the green of the Downs and Epsom Race Course. It seemed that all London was on its way to the races.

At last they arrived and climbed down from the charabanc, mingling with the crowds and catching the excitement of Londoners enjoying a rare day of freedom from drudgery and toil. This was one of the few places where all classes could come and enjoy themselves — although the gentry had their own enclosure and sheltered seats from which to watch the actual races.

But before the off, everyone milled around soaking up the atmosphere, eating, drinking and placing bets. The shouts of the bookies vied with the vendors of hot pies and jellied eels and the smell of friend onions filled the air. Sally and Rose linked arms and joined the smiling crowds.

Rose wanted to place a bet, although Sally tried to dissuade her.

'What's the point of going to the races and not betting?' Rose asked.

Sally was determined not to waste

her hard-earned money, but she helped Rose to try and pick out a likely winner. In the end they chose a horse because of its name — *Rose of Tralee*.

It didn't win of course, but the girls screamed themselves hoarse with encouragement even when it became obvious that *Rose of Tralee* would never catch up with the front runners. When the race was over, they collapsed giggling, leaning on the fence.

Rose wanted to bet again, but Sally managed to persuade her not to risk losing money she could ill afford. They watched another two races, but it wasn't as much fun with no money riding on the outcome. There was still plenty of time before they had to go back to the waiting charabanc so they decided to get a cup of tea and something to eat. They went towards the Royal Box, hoping for a glimpse of the King and Queen. But the crowds were too dense.

As they turned towards the tea tent, Sally caught sight of Harry, Lady

Lazenby's footman. Today he wasn't wearing his fancy footman's livery and for a moment she wasn't sure if it was him. But there was no mistaking that curly hair, the colour of sun-ripened corn — and the smile as he spotted her at the same time and came towards her.

'Never expected to see you today,' he said.

'I'm just as entitled to a day off as you are,' she retorted. She glanced round, pretending to be casual, hoping that Maggie wasn't with him this time. There was no sign of her and she couldn't help feeling pleased. Maybe they weren't walking out together after all. Even so, she knew from the way Maggie had looked at him in the park that she had her eye on him.

Rose tugged at her arm. 'Come on, Sally,' she said.

'We were just going to get some tea,' she said.

'Me too. Mind if I join you?' he crooked his arm in invitation. 'In fact why don't I treat you?'

Sally hesitated.

'Both of you,' he added hastily.

'Thank you, that's very kind,' Rose said, taking his arm and pulling a face at Sally behind his back.

The big marquee was crowded, but Harry managed to find a couple of chairs at the end of one of the long trestle tables. The girls sat down and he went to join the queue.

'You were a bit forward, grabbing his arm like that,' Sally said.

'Well, you weren't doing anything, just standing there with a stupid grin on your face,' Rose retorted, laughing. 'I know you like him and now's your chance to get to know him better.'

'I told you before, Rose. I'm not interested in men!'

Rose laughed even harder. 'You can't fool me. I can tell you're interested in him all right.' She glanced across at the queue and waved at Harry. 'Oh, I know all about your ambitions, but it doesn't hurt to have a little fun.'

'I suppose not. But I don't want him

getting any ideas.'

As Harry came towards them with a tray, her stomach gave a little lurch. There was something about him and she knew that if she wasn't careful she could easily forget her hopes and dreams for an independent future.

He smiled at her as he put the tray down. 'I got some buns as well. This fresh air makes you hungry.' As he passed the cups, he said, 'Oh, forgot the sugar. I'll go and get it.'

'I don't take sugar,' Sally said.

'She's sweet enough already,' Rose joked.

'That's true,' Harry said, sitting down beside her.

Sally felt a hot flush stealing over her. 'You're not working today then?' she said quickly to cover up her confusion.

'It's my day off. I was lucky to be able to come,' he said. 'Her Ladyship's here today with a house party. Some of the servants came down in a separate coach so I tagged along.

'You like horse racing do you?'

'Not really, I'm not a gambler if that's what you mean. But I do like to get out of town now and then. And there's the motors too.' Harry took a sip of his tea and a smile crossed his face.

'Motors? Oh, the motor cars. There seems to be more of them on the roads every day,' Sally said. She was about to add, 'Noisy, smelly things,' but something in his face stopped her. 'Do you like them then?'

'They're the future,' he said. 'And I'm going to have one — one day.'

Sally smiled sympathetically. His dreams seemed to be as lofty as hers — and about as unattainable too. But somehow she believed him. Hadn't she always said that if you wanted something enough and worked for it, you'd get there in the end? 'I'm sure you will,' she said.

He looked hard at her. 'Most people just laugh,' he said. 'Me — a lowly footman.'

'You're no more lowly than me, a milliner. But there's nothing wrong with having dreams and ambitions.'

'It's not just a dream though. I won't be a footman forever. Like I told you before, I've got plans,' he said. 'Just like you.'

So he remembered what they'd talked about before, Sally thought, warming to him. They had so much in common and she was tempted to tell him more about her own idea, but Rose was drumming her fingers on the table. She'd finished her tea and wanted to get back to the race track. There was one more race before the charabanc was due to leave.

'What would you do if you weren't in service?' she asked, pushing back her chair, but longing to prolong the encounter.

'I always wanted to open a shop but now, I'd like to work with motor cars. Sometimes the coachman lets me tinker with the engine of his Lordship's Daimler and I think I've got a feel for it — more than he has anyhow.' Harry stood up too and they started towards the open doorway of the marquee.

As they stepped out into the sunshine a voice accosted Harry.

'I've been looking for you everywhere. Come on, we'll miss the last race.' Maggie slipped her arm through Harry's, giving the two girls a dismissive smile. 'Fancy meeting you two again,' she said.

'We're just off to watch the last race too,' Rose said.

But Sally hung back. 'We'd better find the others,' she said. 'Thank you for the tea. It was nice meeting you again.' She turned away, disappointment welling up in her. He had seemed to be enjoying her company, but as soon as Maggie sidled up with her possessive smirk, it was as if she did not exist. Well, what did she care if Harry was walking out with Maggie? Hadn't she said time and again she wasn't interested in romance? She shouldn't be upset. But she was.

As she hurried away, blinded with tears, her foot caught in a dip in the uneven turf. Pain flashed through her ankle as she stumbled and almost fell.

A hand grasped her firmly by the elbow. 'Whoa there. Are you all right?'

Sally gazed up into a pair of piercing dark eyes and a handsome face which was only marred by the sardonic twist of the lips.

'Well, if isn't the hat girl,' drawled Charles Carey, still holding on to her arm.

Sally felt herself blushing. 'Oh, it's you,' she said, her foolish reaction making her blush even more. She pulled away from him, gasping as she put her weight on her injured ankle and renewed pain brought fresh tears to her eyes.

'So you do remember me?' he said with a smirk. He turned to Rose who was staring open-mouthed. 'It seems your friend isn't going to introduce us. Charles Carey at your service ma'am.'

He took off his hat and made a little bow, then turned to Sally again, saying with what seemed like genuine concern,

'You're hurt, Miss Williams.'

'I'll be all right once we get back to the charabanc. It'll wear off once I'm sitting down.'

'Nonsense, you must allow me to help,' Charles said.

'Really, Mr Carey, it's not necessary.' She turned to her friend. 'Let me lean on you, Rose.'

Charles shrugged and watched as Rose put her arm around Sally and tried to help her to walk. When she gasped with pain again he pushed Rose out of the way. 'This is ridiculous. You must let me.' He picked her up in his arms and strode off towards the area where the carriages and charabancs waited.

'Mr Carey, put me down at once,' Sally said, pushing her hands against his chest.

But he only held her tighter, laughing down at her. 'You are quite safe with me, Miss Williams. That ankle needs attending to.' He turned to Rose. 'I'll take care of your friend and see that she gets home safely. May I suggest you go and inform your party that she will be returning to London with me?'

'I don't know, Sir. Sally, what do you want me to do?' Rose looked from one to the other uncertainly.

Sally didn't want to be alone with Charles Carey, but she had to admit the pain was so bad, she'd never get back to the charabanc unaided. When Charles looked down at her and said, 'I really do want to help — that's all,' she noticed that the sardonic look had completely disappeared from his eyes.

She smiled at her friend. 'It's all right, Rose. You go on. Don't keep them waiting. Come and see me in the morning.'

When Rose had gone, Charles turned to where the carriages of the gentry were waiting.

To her dismay, Sally saw that that one they were approaching bore the Lazenby crest on its door.

A footman sprang to attention and opened the door. Thank goodness it wasn't Harry, Sally thought, as the young man fought to hide his smirk. She would hate him to see her in such an undignified and improper pose.

As Charles Carey set her down inside the carriage she realised that someone was already seated opposite.

'What on earth is going on, Charles — and why is that person in my carriage?' It was Lady Isabelle.

'This young lady is hurt and we are taking her home.' He climbed in and sat beside Sally shouting to the coachman to make haste. He smiled at Sally. 'I believe you have already met my cousin, Miss Williams,' he said. There was a malicious twist to his lips as he spoke and Sally felt herself blushing again.

'It's very kind of your Ladyship,' she whispered.

Lady Isabelle ignored her. 'Charles how dare you! Get that woman out of here this instant.'

'Now, now, Izzy. No tantrums, please. I'm only acting the Good

Samaritan to a lady in distress,' Charles said, laughing as anger sparked in her Ladyship's eyes. 'You don't really want me to throw her out in the middle of nowhere, do you?'

By now the carriage had left the racecourse far behind and the horses were going at spanking pace through open countryside.

Charles left his seat beside Sally and moved to the one opposite, taking Lady Isabelle's hand and kissing it gently. 'Come, sweet cousin, how could I ignore her distress?'

Her Ladyship shrugged him away. 'You are too kind for your own good, Charles. People will take advantage of you,' she said. But she seemed mollified by his attention.

Sally was embarrassed, but thought it better not to try to apologise for fear of making things worse. She looked out of the carriage window at the country-side speeding past, wishing she had been stronger in her protestations. But she had been almost dazed with pain at the time and in no state to argue.

Now there was just a dull throb in her ankle and she felt sure she would have been able to stand on it if she had rested just a little. She was angry with herself too, for allowing herself to get into this situation.

It was all Harry's fault, she told herself. If she hadn't been so upset at the way he'd gone off with Maggie, she would never have tripped over like that. But the damage was done now.

No doubt the story of her being carried in Charles Carey's arms would be spread by the footman and coach-man — servants were notorious gossips. She felt hot at the thought of Harry hearing about it. Not that his opinion of her mattered, she told herself.

The carriage was entering the out-skirts of London and Charles leaned forward to ask where she lived. Sally had to think quickly. It would not do for her to be seen getting out of a carriage in Tanner's Lane. Her reputa-tion would be in shreds. Not that she cared what people thought but she would not upset her mother for anything.

'Could you take me to Madame Chantal's salon, please?' she asked.

'Do you lodge with your employer then?' Charles asked.

Sally evaded the question. 'Madame has been unwell and I have been taking care of her.'

Charles leaned out of the carriage to give the coachman directions. When he sat down again he grinned at Sally. 'Well, I shall know where to find you in future,' he said.'

Lady Isabelle glared at him. 'I fail to see what need you might have in the future for a milliner.' She spat the word 'milliner' as if it were something far worse.

Charles laughed. 'Who knows? I might want to buy you a hat, dear cousin.'

She bit her lip and did not reply. But Sally noticed the whitened knuckles as she clenched her hands on her lap. The famous temper was being kept in check — for a while at least.

'And how is the ankle feeling now, Miss Williams?' Charles leaned forward solicitously, ignoring Lady Isabelle's impatient sigh.

'It is much better now I have rested. I am sure I will be able to walk now. You can set me down here,' Sally said. She didn't want to stay in Charles' company a minute longer than necessary.

Despite his good looks and his undoubted kindness in helping her after her injury, she was uncomfortably aware of an undercurrent of tension between him and his cousin. And, knowing how dependent Madame was on her Ladyship's goodwill, she did not want to be the cause of alienating her and losing her custom.

'Nevertheless, we will deliver you safely to Madame Chantal,' Charles said firmly.

It was with a sigh of relief that Sally recognised the street they had turned into and she was on her feet and out of the carriage almost before it had stopped. Biting her lip against the sudden stab of pain in her ankle, she managed to limp towards the door of the salon.

As Charles made to follow her, she waved him away. 'Do not trouble yourself, Mr Carey. I am quite recovered,' she said and went indoors, closing the door firmly behind her.

5

By the next day the swelling in Sally's ankle had gone down and she was able to put more weight on it. When she'd arrived at the salon the previous evening, her sister had bathed and put a cold compress on it. Then, after making sure that Madame was settled for the night, Jenny had helped her to hobble home.

She had spent a restless night and had woken feeling irritable and out of sorts. She told herself it was the pain of her injured ankle that had kept her awake. But through the long sleepless hours she had gone over and over the events of the previous day trying to analyse the feelings that the handsome Charles Carey had aroused in her.

There was no doubt he was charming and he seemed interested in her. Any girl would be flattered. But despite his good looks and his charm, he wasn't Harry. Then she remembered him smiling down into Maggie's laughing eyes as she clung to his arm. She swallowed the lump in her throat and asked herself why she was so upset. What was a mere footman to her anyway? Besides she hardly knew him.

She was replacing the bandage on her ankle when her mother came through from the scullery. 'You need to rest that,' she said.

'I'm all right, Mum. It doesn't hurt so much today,' Sally replied, standing up and gently testing her weight on the injured foot. She bit her lip, but managed to hobble across the room.

'Good job it's Sunday and you don't have to go to work,' said Ada.

'I must go and see Madame though. I promised to look in and see if she needed anything.'

'Why don't you send Jenny? She managed all right yesterday.'

'I'll see how I feel after dinner.' Sally sat down at the kitchen table and began to peel the potatoes her mother had brought in. As she worked she spoke about Madame and the salon, praising her little sister's care of her employer. She didn't want to talk about her outing. But she couldn't avoid the subject for long.

'Is Rose coming round today?' Ada asked.

'She's going out with her young man.'

Sally smiled but the smile disappeared when her mother said, 'It's about time you got yourself a young man, too.'

'I'm not interested. You know I want a career first.' Sally spoke quickly, but she could feel the hot tide washing up her neck and she hoped her mother wouldn't notice her confusion.

Ada went on chopping carrots for the stew. 'You spend too much time with that old woman. A young girl like you should be out enjoying herself on her day off.'

'Madame has been very good to me.

Besides, if I don't keep the business going, I won't have a job.' Sally was reluctant to let her mother know how much she had enjoyed the past week, doing the books, keeping the orders coming. She felt proud of her achievement, but she thought Ada might think she was getting above herself.

'You've been good to her too. I just hope she appreciates all you've done for her,' Ada said, adding the carrots and onions to the mutton stew which was already simmering on the range. 'Anyway, I've said it before — you could get a job anywhere with your skills.'

'And I've said before — I won't leave Madame in the lurch. If I ever do leave, it will be to open my own salon — not that there's much chance of that.'

'Well, we know why that is, don't we!' Ada pressed her lips together and began to wipe the table vigorously.

Sally didn't reply. Despite her mother's oft-repeated remark it was up to her what she did with her own money, she knew that Ada did not approve of her using her hard-won savings to prop up her employer's ailing business.

After dinner, Sally set off with Jenny through the drowsing Sunday streets to Madame's salon. The throb in her ankle had subsided to a dull ache now and although she still limped a little, she was able to ignore the pain as she listened to her younger sister's bright chatter. She smiled down into the eager face and remembered it was not just for herself that she was so determined to make good.

When she had her own salon, she would take Jenny on as an apprentice. None of her family would ever suffer want again once she was successful. Her daydreams served to push away the painful memory of Harry's so obvious enjoyment of Maggie's company and the disturbing image of Charles Carey's sardonic smile.

They reached the salon and Jenny ran ahead to hold the door open. Sally suppressed a gasp of surprise when she saw that Madame was not only out of bed, but downstairs at her desk. She was studying the sheaf of papers in her hand.

Sally smiled tentatively. 'Madame, you must be feeling better.' She took a step forward, trying to ignore the tightness of her employer's lips. 'Are you sure you're well enough to be up and working?'

Madame's face was ashen. 'It's a good job I came down. Who knows what you've been up to in my absence?' She slapped a hand against the pile of invoices. 'How dare you go through my private papers? What gives you — an apprentice — the right?'

Her voice trailed away and Sally noticed that beads of sweat stood out on her forehead.

She did not think it was the right moment to remind Madame that she was no longer an apprentice. 'I'm sorry, Madame. I did what I thought was right in the circumstances.' She took a step forward. 'You really should still be resting. Let me . . . '

'No. I'm quite all right,' Madame stood up and pushed her chair back. 'I trusted you, Sally, but you have shown a complete disregard for my wishes.'

Sally started to protest, to justify her actions. but Madame held out a hand as if to push her away. 'Please go. We'll discuss your future employment, if any, tomorrow. Please be here at your usual time.'

It was useless to argue. 'Very well, Madame.' Sally took Jenny's hand and within seconds they were out on the street again.

'Why is she so cross?' Jenny asked. 'Have I done something wrong?'

'It's nothing to do with you, love. Don't worry about it. She's still not well. I'll talk to her tomorrow,' Sally said.

She hoped that once Madame realised that she had acted in the interests of the business as well as her own, she would forgive her interference. But Madame Chantal was a strong independent woman who would not take kindly to what she saw as charity. Sally understood. Wasn't she like that, too?

It would be hard to start all over again though. Even if she did manage to get another job, it would take time to replenish her savings.

As they reached the end of Tanner's Lane she turned to Jenny, 'Run along home, love,' she said. 'Tell Mum I'll be in later.' She couldn't face her mother at the moment — the questions, the recriminations.

'Where you goin' then?' Jenny asked.

'Never you mind. I'm just going for a walk.' She hobbled away before Jenny could ask any more questions.

Her unthinking footsteps took her through the narrow terraced streets in the direction of the park and she wondered whether Rose would still be there waiting for Thomas. She needed someone to talk to. But even before she reached the bandstand she could see that they'd already left. The musicians had gone and the park attendant was folding and stacking the chairs.

The park was still crowded on this bright Sunday afternoon and Sally craned her neck, hoping for a glimpse of her friend. After a few minutes she turned away. Even if she saw Rose it would hardly be fair to intrude on her and Thomas. The young couple had little enough chance to spend time together.

Sally walked along the edge of the lake, lingering to watch a group of children sailing toy boats. Some had taken off their shoes and stockings to splash at the water's edge, watched by indulgent parents or nannies. On the far side of the lake, horse riders cantered under the trees and there were several open carriages parading the wide gravel paths, their occupants bowing and smiling, showing off their finery.

It was a pleasant scene, but Sally scarcely took it in, her mind busy with tomorrow's interview with Madame

Chantal. Whatever she might feel in justification of her actions, she had to admit that she had been presumptuous and that Madame had a perfect right to be angry.

However ill Madame had been, she should have been consulted. Sally suppressed a pang of guilt, for deep down she knew that her employer would never have agreed — especially to her using her own money to keep the business afloat. It smacked far too much of charity. She would just have to cling on to the hope that she would eventually be forgiven. But it was a vain hope: Madame was a proud and independent woman.

Lost in thought, Sally jumped when a voice said, 'What are you doing here all alone then? Waiting for your fancy man?'

She whirled round indignantly to confront Harry and Maggie. 'I don't know what you mean,' she said.

'Yes, you do.' Harry's voice was harsh, his lips twisted in a contemptuous grimace. There was no trace of the friendly open face he'd shown her yesterday. 'I saw you after we left, getting all cosy with her Ladyship's cousin.'

Maggie laughed and Sally felt her face flaming. 'I had a fall and Mr Carey helped me — not that it's any business of yours,' Sally snapped.

'Come on, Harry,' Maggie said, taking his arm.

But he pulled away and turned back to Sally. 'You're right — it's none of my business.' His voice was less harsh now. 'It's just — I didn't think you were that sort of girl.'

'I'm not. I didn't . . . ' Sally wasn't usually lost for words. Anyway, why did she feel the need to defend herself? He was nothing to her.

That's what she told herself anyway as she stuck her chin out and started to walk away, still limping a little. His voice followed her, gentle, almost imploring. 'Sally, I don't want you to get hurt. Just watch out . . . '

Tears welled up in her eyes and she turned back, suddenly anxious to explain, to make him see how wrong he was about her. But Maggie called to him impatiently and he shrugged and turned away.

Sally carried on walking. Maggie's laugh followed her, but she did not turn round. If she saw Harry laughing too it would break her heart.

6

The pain in Sally's ankle was worse now. She had walked too far, but pride would not let her take a rest until she was out of Harry and Maggie's sight. Her stubbornness kept her going until she reached the other side of the lake. Spotting an empty bench, she sank onto it and bent to massage her now swollen ankle.

It was tempting to unbutton her boot and ease the pressure, but she knew she'd never get it done up again. She glanced about her, wondering how she'd get home. She had no money for a cab.

She sighed and leaned against the back of the bench, closing her eyes against the glare of the lowering sun. Maybe if she rested a while, she'd be able to hobble home. Eyes still closed, she relived the encounter with Harry, wishing she had never set eyes on Charles Carey. If he hadn't been at the races yesterday, things might have turned out very differently.

'Miss Williams, I hardly thought I would be fortunate enough to see you today. I thought you would be at home resting after your accident.'

Sally's eyes flew open and she sat upright, smoothing her skirt and trying to avoid Charles Carey's sardonic gaze. He seemed to pop up everywhere these days. What possible interest could a gentleman like him have in a lowly milliner?

She shifted to the end of the bench as, without invitation or apology, he sat down beside her, pointing his silver-topped cane at her foot. 'The ankle — it is better, I trust?'

'Much better, thank you, Sir,' she replied. 'It was just a slight sprain.' Not for the world would she admit to him the pain which now throbbed along her whole foot and up into her calf.

'Your friends have deserted you today

it seems. A pretty girl like you should not spend your Sundays alone.' His dark eyes twinkled. 'Or perhaps you have quarrelled with your young man — is that why you sit alone looking so sad?'

Sally was indignant. Why did everyone persist in thinking that a girl's troubles could only stem from a man? It was true she had been thinking of Harry, but her depression stemmed more from apprehension about the coming interview with Madame Chantal.

She took a deep breath. 'I am not sad, I was merely thinking, trying to solve a problem . . . '

'Ah, so there is a problem. Why don't you tell me all about it? Perhaps I can help.' He moved closer and took her hand.

'Mr Carey, I hardly think the problems of a 'hat girl' could interest you.' She tried to snatch her hand away, but the pressure of his fingers tightened.

'Oh, but they do,' he said.

She tried to protest again, but she saw that the sardonic twist to his mouth had disappeared and his eyes were serious now, seeming to reflect genuine concern. 'Just tell me,' he said softly.

She hesitated, then spoke tentatively. 'I have done something I should not . . . ' She paused thinking he would laugh. But his gaze remained serious and he nodded her to continue. 'My employer, Madam Chantal, is very angry with me. I do not know if I still have a job even . . . ' A sob caught in her throat.

Charles patted her hand. 'I am sure it cannot be too dreadful.'

'But it is. I disobeyed her, abused her trust. I took upon myself . . . ' The tears fell faster as Sally, almost for the first time, realised how her actions would look to an outsider.

She had been so proud of herself, so sure that she was acting in Madame's best interest when all the time it was her own interests that had been paramount. How would she ever make amends?

Under Charles sympathetic probing the story poured out. She found herself not only telling him how she had tried to save Madame's business, but also confessing her hopes and ambitions for the future.

'My dear young lady, there is no shame in being ambitious, to want to better your station in life. And you have talent — I have heard my cousin say so,' Charles said.

Sally gazed up at him through eyes clouded with tears. She suddenly became aware that his arm was round her and that her head was almost resting on his chest.

As she made to pull away, he raised a hand and wiped away the tear that still trembled on her lashes. 'There is nothing to cry about, my dear.'

'But Madame is so angry — and I don't blame her. I went about things the wrong way.

'Never mind Madame. She is old and

would have had to give up soon anyway. You have your future ahead of you — and I can help.'

'But how? I do not think making ladies' hats is a man's business.' Sally managed a little smile.

'Any business needs capital — enough to get you started, to rent premises and such.'

'But I could not take money, Sir. It would not be right.' Sally could imagine her mother's look of horror if she agreed to such a thing.

'It would be an investment, my dear. A business arrangement only.'

The sardonic grin was back. 'Besides, it would not be my money. Like you, I have no capital of my own. But I do have friends, family . . . '

'Not Lady Lazenby. She would never . . . '

'Maybe not. But her husband . . . ' Charles nodded thoughtfully.

'His Lordship is extremely wealthy.'

Sally could not imagine why a rich lord would consider investing in such a small venture — especially one run by a woman. But Charles seemed confident.

She still had her doubts as to the wisdom of accepting help from a man she scarcely knew. But the future did not seem quite so bleak now. Charles' confidence in her ability had helped to restore her faith in herself.

But she was still cautious. She pulled away from him and said, 'I will have to think about it, Sir. Who knows, Madame may relent and allow me to continue working for her. But I thank you for your offer of help — and for listening to my troubles.' She stood up, rather unsteadily and although the pain still throbbed in her ankle it had eased sufficiently for her to take a few steps.

Evening had crept upon them and the park was almost deserted. Charles stood too and caught at her hand. 'Please believe me. I really want to help you.'

'I will consider your offer, but I must go home now.'

They walked towards the park gates, Sally stumbling occasionally. Charles took her arm and she would have pulled away, but she realised she needed his support. He hailed a cab and gave the cabbie directions to Tanner's Lane.

She hoped he would not try to accompany her. But he paid the cabbie, helped her into the seat and raised his hat. 'Meet me here next Sunday at the same time. I will let you know what his Lordship says and we can discuss our future plans.'

Future plans, thought Sally as she propped her aching foot up on the seat opposite and went over the encounter in her mind. She couldn't help feeling excited — her own salon at last. She just knew it would be a success and she'd be able to pay Charles Carey back. She didn't want to be beholden to him for longer than necessary.

A few months ago she would never even have contemplated accepting help. But that was before everything had gone wrong for Madame. She had done what she thought was right at the time, but her reward was to be threatened with unemployment. Well, she didn't need Madame Chantal any more. She would manage alone.

As the cab deposited her at the end of Tanner's Lane, a small voice insisted that she wasn't really managing alone, was she? And there was that other voice in her head — her mother's. 'Don't expect something for nothing. Just ask yourself, what does he want from you?'

She thrust the thought away as she pushed open the front door, plastering a smile on her face before entering the crowded kitchen.

The children were at the table having their supper and Ada, as usual, was busy at the range. She turned round, a cloth in her hand. 'You're late, love. I was just beginning to worry. Is your ankle all right?'

'Much better,' Sally lied. 'I went to the park, sat by the lake. It was too nice to stay indoors.'

'Did you see Rose? She came round earlier?'

'I missed her. But I bumped into a couple of friends. That's why I was late.' Sally had never lied to her mother before, but she could imagine the disapproving frown if she confessed who she had really been with.

Ada had a deep distrust of the gentry and, Sally thought, she was probably right. She sighed and joined her brothers and sisters at the table, reached out for a slice of bread.

Sitting here in the shabby kitchen, surrounded by her loving family, her conversation with Charles Carey now seemed like a dream. He hadn't meant it, was just trying to be kind, she told herself.

But as she tried to get to sleep later that night she realised that kindness had not been the emotion she had seen in those dark brooding eyes. She had to acknowledge that whatever help he gave her, he would expect payment in return. And she wasn't sure if it was a price she was prepared to pay.

7

Sally approached the salon hesitantly, rehearsing the words that she hoped would convince Madame Chantal that she had been acting in her best interests. She had never really meant to usurp her employer's authority and had always known that once Madame recovered from her illness they would have to revert to their original relationship — Madame was the boss, she the lowly assistant. But so long as she still had a job, she didn't care.

The reality of life in the Williams household had asserted itself as soon as she had come downstairs that morning. The sight of her mother, red-faced and red-armed, up to her elbows in steam and suds as she prodded the piles of washing that helped to put food on the table, her small brothers and sister in their shabby clothes munching on bread and dripping before going off to school, had brought home to her the impossibility of her dream.

She had to hold on to her job somehow. Besides, how could she have believed that Charles Carey's offer to set her up in her own business had been without strings? And why had she even contemplated accepting?

She knew the answer, of course. She'd been hurt by Harry's accusations and even more hurt at the sight of Maggie acting so possessively. She stood no chance with him and she wondered why she minded so much. After all, they'd only met a few times and she told herself she hardly knew him. Why did his opinion matter so much?

Her thoughts churned as she hurried through the busy streets, her steps slowing as she neared the salon and she rehearsed what she would say to Madame Chantal.

The coming interview would not be easy, but she would have to swallow her pride, apologise and hope Madame would understand. Whatever happened, she would definitely not be meeting Charles Carey in the park next Sunday.

She opened the salon door, fixed a smile on her face and said, 'Good morning, Madame. How are you today?'

Madame looked up from her desk. 'I'm very well, thank you — quite well enough to attend to her own business now.' Her voice was cool, her lips tight. But at least she didn't seem quite as angry as she had yesterday.

'I'm pleased you're better,' Sally said. 'What would you like me to do today?' She held her breath, waiting for Madame to tell her she no longer had a job. But to her relief Madame just shrugged.

'I see from the book that you have promised Miss Willoughby's hat for Wednesday so perhaps you'd better work on that.' Her voice was cool, emotionless.

Sally swallowed the lump in her

throat and took a step forward. 'Madame, please, let me . . . '

'I don't wish to discuss it. I realise you probably thought you were acting for the best. I should thank you for looking after me while I was ill. But, Sally, I should have been consulted, I would never have agreed . . . '

'I did what I thought was right at the time.'

Madame's voice softened. 'I know you did. I have looked through the books and I know that if it weren't for you I would no longer be in business. But I am in debt still — to you. It is not a position an employer wishes to find herself in!'

'I don't mind. Besides, I don't consider it a debt. I was keeping myself in employment too.' It was a justification that Sally thought Madame would understand.

'We'll say no more about it then. Go up now and get on with Miss Willoughby's hat.'

As she turned towards the stairs

Madame's voice followed her. 'Rest assured, Sally, I will repay every penny.'

Sally did not reply. In the work room, as she laid out her tools and materials, she reflected that it was most unlikely she would recoup her savings.

Despite being up and at her desk, Madame still looked frail, her cheeks pale, dark shadows under her eyes and a faint trembling in her hands.

It would be some time before she was fit enough to resume the fine stitching for which she was noted — if ever. And if she insisted on reverting to her old way of dealing with the business side it would not be long before Chantal's was in trouble again.

As she worked on the hat for Miss Willoughby, the spectre of unemployment still hung over her, and Sally could not help thinking about Charles Carey's offer. It was tempting.

She would be able to do things her way and she just knew she had the talent and the business sense to make a success of it.

And she was sure she could take over the customers who had come to rely on her during Madame's illness. But she knew that all the time Madame continued to struggle along, she would never set up in opposition to her. Madame Chantal had taught her so much and in many ways, despite their recent difference, she was more a friend than an employer.

★ ★ ★

As the week went on, the tension between Sally and Madame Chantal began to thaw.

Miss Willoughby's hat was completed to Madame's satisfaction — and more importantly, the client's.

She was delighted with Sally's creation. 'I am so glad my friend, Miss Davenport, told me about you,' she said. She was accompanied by another friend today and she too was most impressed — so impressed that she ordered a new hat for a society wedding she would be attending in the autumn. To Sally's surprise, Madame included her in the discussions about the client's needs.

When colours and style had been decided upon, Madame said, 'My assistant will draw up some sketches for your approval. Would you like her to bring them to you or can you call in next week?'

The new client, Mrs Bailey, smiled. 'I'll call in.'

When she had gone Sally said, 'Thank you, Madame. I'll do my best.'

'I know you will, Sally. Your ability as a milliner has never been in question.' She returned to her desk and began to write in the order book, her shoulders rigid.

Sally slowly mounted the stairs to the work room. Madame was a long way from truly forgiving her for her interference, but at least she still had a job.

As the weeks passed, they settled into a routine, Sally sketching designs, while

Madame dealt with the customers and the book keeping. But Sally was worried when Madame insisted that she would continue to do the fine work for which she was noted. She just would not admit that her eyesight was no longer up to it and she often made mistakes.

Sally dared not point it out to her, especially as they had almost recovered their old easy relationship. She did not want to spoil things again.

When Madame began to murmur about needing another apprentice, Sally grew alarmed. The business had not recovered to the extent that they could think about taking anyone else on. But she couldn't interfere. Besides, she knew Madame would not listen.

She had to think of something though, and when Madame raised the subject again, she said, 'What a pity my little sister is not old enough for an apprenticeship. I know she would love to learn millinery.'

'Yes, Jenny's a good girl,' Madame

agreed. 'She worked very hard when she was looking after me.'

'Do you really think we need someone straight away?'

'We have quite a few orders now and someone has to do the steaming and blocking, the sweeping up and sorting the materials — all the things you used to do, Sally.'

'I have a suggestion, Madame,' Sally bit her lip, knowing that Madame could easily take offence again.

'Well, speak up, girl.'

'Why not let Jenny come in and help out after school and maybe on Saturdays? I could teach her and then, when she leaves school you could think about taking her on as a full-time apprentice.' Sally held her breath, letting it out in a sigh of relief as Madame nodded slowly.

'I'll give her a chance. Let's hope she's a little more amenable, not so strong-willed as her sister. I don't think I could cope with two of you.' Madame spoke sharply, but there was a suggestion of a smile, quickly suppressed.

'Thank you, Madam,' Sally said quietly.

Jenny was a quick learner, eager to please and grateful for the chance to help her mother and older sister by contributing to the household. Business continued to pick up and Madame's health improved daily.

As for Sally, she was happy to be back in Madame's good books and to have the chance to do the work she loved — designing. But she had not completely given up the dream of owning her own business one day. She just accepted that it would take longer than she'd thought.

The fleeting thought that she could have had it sooner if she'd accepted Charles Carey's help was soon dismissed.

It would be no real achievement if she did not do it on her own.

She tried not to think that if it had been Harry making the offer she would have felt differently. But he was only a footman and besides, he didn't care about her. She told herself she wasn't a bit jealous of Maggie. A footman and a maid were right for each other. She had set her sights on a bigger prize — her own business.

She remembered Harry telling her he would not always be a footman and indulged in a daydream of them starting a business together. It would never happen and now that the pile of coins in the biscuit tin on the dresser shelf had started to mount up once more, Sally knew that one day she would achieve her own dream — by her own efforts. It would take time, but she would get there in the end.

★　★　★

Towards the end of the summer relations between Sally and her employer had improved still further. Some of their clients had paid their outstanding bills thanks to the reminders Sally had sent out. But Madame refused to set up a system of monthly invoices followed by reminders. 'I trust my clients,' she said. 'I've had no trouble in the past.'

But she had, although Sally bit her lip and did not say what was on her mind. As Madame constantly reminded her these days, she was the boss. She did not want to force a confrontation and she knew she had to keep her job until she had managed to start saving again.

The first time Madame handed her an envelope containing more than her weekly wage, she had tried to protest. The business couldn't afford it yet. But Madame's back had become rigid. 'This is the first instalment of my debt to you. I said I would repay you — and I will.'

Sally relented knowing she would feel the same in Madame's position. They were both proud and stubborn.

8

Sally and Rose were walking in the park one Sunday in early September, Rose scuffing her toes in the wet leaves, upset because she had not heard from Thomas. The band had gone away on tour for the rest of the summer and she was missing him.

'Not even a postcard,' she said. 'Maybe he doesn't love me at all.'

'Of course he does, silly,' Sally told her. 'Some men aren't good at writing letters. Anyway, it won't be long now — only another couple of weeks.'

'Thirteen days actually,' Rose said, a smile lighting up her eyes.

'At least you have someone,' Sally said.

Rose laughed. 'Thought you weren't interested in romance, thought you wanted to be a business woman.'

'I don't see why you can't have both,'

Sally said, thinking of Harry and his determination not to remain a footman forever.

'I don't see why you'd want both,' her friend replied. 'Besides, it isn't done.'

Sally shrugged and gave up. Rose would never understand. They walked along in silence for a few minutes, Sally lost in thought. She was beginning to wonder if she had done the right thing in avoiding Charles Carey. If she had taken him up on his offer she would have her own salon by now.

She knew it was disloyal to think like this. But although Madame appeared to have put the past misunderstandings behind her, the business was not doing as well as it should — and Sally knew the reason.

She just didn't know what to do about it though. She did know, however, that she could not involve the handsome Mr Carey in her future plans. He was far too dangerous.

Lost in thought she did not hear the

thunder of hooves until the horse was almost upon her. She jumped back in alarm, grabbing at Rose's arm. As if she had conjured him in her thoughts, Charles reined in his horse and leant from the saddle, laughing.

'Miss Williams, we meet again,' he said, dismounting smoothly and taking her hand.

She snatched it away, glaring at him. 'How dare you frighten us like that,' she snapped. 'You should have more control over your animal.'

He raised a sardonic eyebrow. 'My apologies for frightening you. I thought you had more spirit than to be scared of a horse. Besides, I can assure you I was in perfect control.'

He reached for her hand again, his eyes softening. 'I am truly sorry, It was just that I saw you from the other side of the park and thought you were about to walk away. I had to speak to you. It seems such a long time since I last saw you here. I thought perhaps you were trying to avoid me.'

It was true of course and Sally flushed, remembering their last encounter and her promise to meet him again. Conscious that he still had her hand in his, she pulled away. 'I do not have time to walk in the park these days. I am a working girl after all,' she said.

'Oh, then you managed to keep your job. I am pleased for you, though . . . ' The grin was back. 'It is a pity in a way. I was looking forward to doing business with you.' He touched his riding crop to his hat and re-mounted.

As he rode away he looked back. 'The offer is still open, if ever you should need it,' he said.

Sally watched him canter across the grass, her face still burning. She turned as Rose pulled at her sleeve. 'What was he talking about? What business?'

'Nothing. It was a foolish notion.'

'How could you have anything to do with a man like that?' Rose asked, her round honest face screwed up in a worried frown.

'What do you mean — a man like

that?' Sally asked. 'He has been very kind to me.'

'I know he helped when you were hurt at the races but . . . ' Rose hesitated, then blurted out, 'He has a bad reputation — I've heard things. Besides, why would he be kind unless he wanted something in return? Men of his class . . . ' her voice trailed away and she stared miserably at her friend.

Sally knew that Rose was concerned for her and she tried to smile reassuringly. 'You've no need to worry. I must admit I was tempted for a while when he offered to help me set up my own business. But I realised it would not be right. And now that Madame and I are working so well together, it no longer matters.'

They continued their walk, Sally still shaken by the encounter with a man that, despite everything, she could not get out of her thoughts. It was hard not to be flattered by his obvious attraction to her, especially when the man whose attention she did crave was seemingly unaware of her presence.

She shook her head, took Rose's arm and said, 'What about you and Thomas? Have you named the day yet?'

Rose smiled. 'We have decided to wait till next spring. It will give us time to save up for a nice wedding.'

'I'll make you a really special hat for the occasion. In fact, I'll make your dress too,' Sally said.

'Oh, that'll be wonderful. And of course you'll be my bridesmaid, won't you?'

'You don't have to ask,' Sally said. But her mind wasn't really on her friend as she went on to talk about the items she had started to collect for her trousseau. Although she had managed to erase the encounter with Charles from her mind, she was still preoccupied with the dilemma of Madame Chantal and the threat to the salon.

As they reached the park gates, Rose pulled at her arm. 'Look, isn't that Harry?'

Sally looked across the lake, pretending she could not see him. She had no wish to be polite to him and his lady friend. But Rose waved and called out, 'Harry, over here.'

He hunched his shoulder and carried on walking. Rose ran towards him and grabbed his arm. 'We haven't seen you for a while.'

At least Maggie wasn't with him today, Sally thought as she pasted a smile on her face and forced herself to greet him. 'And how is Maggie?' she asked.

She recoiled as he turned to her with a snarl. 'You should know better than anyone how she is, since you were responsible for her losing her job,' he said.

'Me? I don't know what you're talking about. I didn't know she'd lost her job. What happened?' Sally was horrified. She was jealous of Maggie it was true, but she would never have done anything to hurt her.

She tried to recall the last time she had seen Maggie and if she could have said anything in Lady Lazenby's presence that would have inflamed her

Ladyship's notorious temper. But the last time her Ladyship had visited the salon she had been accompanied by a different maid. Now Sally realised why.

Harry was ranting furiously and it was a moment before she could take in what he was saying. ' . . . and she stuck up for you, said that Carey was taking advantage of you. Her Ladyship was furious and said she had expected more loyalty from a personal maid. Dismissed her on the spot — and it's your fault.' He started to walk away in disgust, but Sally followed him.

'I don't understand. Please believe me. Why were Maggie and Lady Lazenby talking about me in the first place? Was it something to do with the hat I designed?'

'Hats! Is that all you can think about?' He almost spat. 'This had nothing to do with hats and all to do with her Ladyship's jealousy. Didn't you know she was having an affair with Carey? And then he took up with you . . . '

'But he's supposed to be her cousin,' Sally stammered, the blood draining from her face as she took in his next words. 'But he didn't . . . I didn't . . . '

Harry gave a short laugh. 'Don't try to deny it. I just saw you together. He was all over you. It's a pity you have to drag your friend into your little schemes,' he said glancing at Rose.

Sally stretched out her hand. 'Please — listen to me.'

But it was too late. Harry was striding away and she did not have the strength to follow and try to explain how wrong he was.

A few days later she was still smarting over Harry's accusation and she cursed the day she had ever set eyes on Charles Carey. She thought of writing to Harry to try to explain, but she didn't think it would do any good.

Besides, he didn't care about her, not to mention that he held her responsible for Maggie being dismissed. Why should he believe her when he had seen her in intimate conversation with Carey and not once, but several times?

Besides, her worries about her reputation paled beside the concern over Madame Chantal's business. It was no use putting it off. She would have to speak out and risk upsetting her employer again. Miss Davenport had been very tactful about a mistake, but Sally knew if it had been one of their more outspoken clients such as Lady Isabelle, it could have spelled trouble for the salon.

If nothing was done about it, the same thing was bound to occur again.

Since Madame had regained her strength she was determined to regain control of every aspect of the business and that meant doing the fine work for which she had become famous, despite her failing eyesight.

Sally had realised the problem and had tried tactfully to supervise her employer's work. In the guise of being helpful she made sure that Madame had the right colour thread and that she attached the correct trimmings. But she had been out on an errand and not noticed this time. Fortunately Miss Davenport had accepted the apology and not withdrawn her custom.

Since then Sally had been more vigilant, but her patience was often tried as Madame's irritation found expression in sarcastic comments. At such times she bit her lip and told herself it was the for the good of the business.

The weather had turned cold and wet as the days grew shorter The work room was dark at the best of times, but today they had to light the gas in mid afternoon. As the room brightened, Sally glanced over to where Madame sat at the bench, trying to thread a needle with fine peach coloured silk. After watching several fruitless attempts she felt bound to intervene.

Never mind being tactful she thought as she offered to help.

'I can manage,' Madame snapped. But after another attempt, she threw the needle down and rubbed her eyes.

'There's nothing wrong with me — I'm just a little tired,' she said.

Sally picked up the needle and threaded the silk through the eye, pausing before she handed it back to Madame. 'Is this for her Ladyship?' she asked, picking up the design.

'Yes, though why she wants such a light colour for this season I don't know,' Madame said.

'This ivory colour is very fashionable just now,' Sally said. 'Is that what she specified?'

'Of course.'

'Then why are you using peach silk to sew the trimming on?' Sally asked gently.

'I'm not. It's this gas light that tints everything. You know I prefer to work in natural light, but this must be finished.

Sally did not point out that Madame had already started to use the wrong colour before she had switched the lights on. She just fetched the spool of ivory silk and re-threaded the needle.

This can't go on, she thought with a

sigh. She couldn't watch Madame's every move. She had her own work to do.

With relief she heard the door open and turned to greet Jenny, who had just finished school for the day. Showing her sister what jobs needed to be done and chatting about her day at school served to distract her from her problems. But she knew she could not ignore them for long.

9

Sally had been avoiding Rose, telling herself it was to allow her friend to spend more time with Thomas. In fact she dreaded a lecture. After their last encounter with Harry, Rose had berated her for getting involved with Charles Carey. 'It's your own fault,' she said. 'You can't blame Harry for thinking the worst.'

She had told Rose sharply to mind her own business, but now she saw that her friend was right. Sally was not entirely blameless for the misunderstanding. She decided to call at Rose's after work and apologise. She only hoped she would be forgiven for her harsh words.

Her relief was overwhelming when her friend opened the door and welcomed her with her usual open smile.

'I've missed you, Sally. Come in.'

Sally followed her into the cosy kitchen where Rose's parents and young brother were eating their evening meal. She hesitated at the door. 'I've come at the wrong time. I'll come back later,' she said.

'Don't be silly. Sit down and have a cup of tea,' Mrs Parker said, going to the dresser to fetch another cup.

'No thanks. I just wanted a quick word with Rose.' How could she say what needed to be said in front of her friend's family?

Rose seemed to sense her dilemma. 'It's all right, Mum, I've finished. Is it all right if I walk up the road with Sally?'

'Don't be too long then.'

Rose grabbed her coat off the hook on the back door and followed Sally out into the street.

'Are you not seeing Thomas this evening then?' Sally knew he was back in town after the band's tour had ended.

'He's on duty tonight so we've got plenty of time to talk.' Rose said, linking her arm through Sally's.

It was almost dark and there was a chilly wind, but Sally ignored it. She was just pleased she still had the warmth of Rose's friendship. She hesitated, then blurted out. 'I've been such a fool, Rose. You were right about Charles Carey — after all, why should he want to help me just for nothing?'

'He's a charming man, Sally. Anyone could be forgiven for being taken in by him.'

'The awful thing is . . . ' Sally hesitated. 'I wasn't really taken in. I knew what sort of man he was. How could I have been so stupid?'

'You weren't though, were you? You told him you didn't need his help.'

'I was tempted though, Rose. I could have had my own salon. It was everything I dreamed of.'

'At what price though?'

Sally bit her lip. It was a question she'd asked herself often over the past months. She turned to her friend. 'You won't tell anyone, will you? It's bad enough Harry thinking the worst. I couldn't bear it if Madam Chantal ever found out.'

She choked on a sob. 'That woman taught me everything I know. If it weren't for her I wouldn't know how to trim a hat, let alone run a business. How could I ever have thought of setting up in opposition to her?'

Rose squeezed her arm. 'Of course I won't tell. Besides, you've been a good friend to Madame. Look how you cared for her when she was ill. You've more than repaid her. And as for Harry, he'll come round in time.'

'I don't think so. He blames me for his girlfriend losing her job. Suppose she can't get another position?'

'Don't you worry about Maggie. I saw her recently and she told me she's got a job in the factory next door to where I work. She's earning more money and she seems a lot happier these days. Besides, she's not Harry's girlfriend, although I think she'd like to be. She told me they only went out and about together because they had the same day off.'

Sally should have been pleased. But she only felt renewed despair. She had forfeited any chance with Harry now so what did it matter if he was free? They reached the turning to Tanner's Lane and she released Rose's arm. 'I'm sorry to burden you with my troubles. Thanks for listening and thanks for still being my friend.'

Rose gave her a little push and laughed. 'It'll take more than a disagreement over a man to spoil our friendship.'

When Sally arrived at the salon the following day she stood in the doorway for a moment, noticing how frail Madame looked, hunched over her desk and squinting at the columns of figures in the big black ledger.

Fresh shame washed over her as she realised how callous she had been trying to take over the business while

Madame was ill, imposing her own plans and ideas when they were not wanted. She would make it up to her she thought, resolving to try even harder to be patient with her employer's failings.

It was hard though, especially as the more her eyesight deteriorated, the more impatient Madame became — and the more intolerant of Sally's help. She was determined to carry on working, even at the risk of losing clients.

Sally covered for her as tactfully as she could, but it was only a matter of time before something went wrong.

She was in the back room showing Jenny how she wanted the felt blocked for a new hat when she heard raised voices coming from the salon. Knowing that Madame resented any interference, she carried on talking to her sister until it became impossible to ignore the furore.

'I might have known it would be Lady Lazenby kicking up a fuss,' she said, going to the door of the salon.

She entered the salon slowly, dreading a confrontation with their ill-tempered client. When her Ladyship had resumed her patronage of Chantal's, Madame had been overjoyed. Influential society ladies were the breath of life to her business and personal recommendation made all the difference. Sally wasn't so sure.

For all her wealth and influence, she thought Lady Isabelle was more trouble than she was worth. And, as she heard the distinctly unladylike language being thrown at Madame, Sally knew she was right. She marched into the salon, prepared to do battle.

Lady Lazenby was holding the beautiful hat that Jenny had delivered to her a day or two earlier. But it was no longer beautiful. The net veil was shredded and hanging in tatters, the ostrich feathers crushed and broken. The hat box lay in a corner of the salon where her Ladyship had thrown it.

As Sally watched, Lady Lazenby tore at the hat, scattering the trimming across the salon. 'That's what I think of your so-called fine workmanship,' she shrieked. 'How dare you present me with this — this — rubbish.'

Madame shrank back in her chair as the remains of the hat were thrown on the desk.

Lady Lazenby's voice dropped to a hiss. 'You'll get no more business from me — and I shall make sure that none of my friends patronises you ever again.'

Sally came into the room and stood behind Madame, her hand on her employer's shoulder. 'What is the trouble, your Ladyship?' she asked in a calm voice, as if she could not see the destruction the woman had inflicted.

'Trouble — can't you see for yourself? Nothing is right. The feathers are the wrong colour and I did not specify a veil. It looks ridiculous. I'd be a laughing stock if I wore that — thing.' Her ladyship's voice rose again.

'I've said I'm sorry,' Madame stammered.

Before Lady Lazenby could start

ranting again, Sally stepped forward. 'I am sure if you had pointed out the error, it could have been put right. Now . . . ' Her gaze swept the salon, taking in the ripped and torn remnants of weeks of work. She walked past her and opened the salon door. 'Good day, your Ladyship. I think you had better leave — and may I say it has *not* been a pleasure serving you!'

'What did you say? How dare you!' The blue eyes were like chips of ice.

'And how dare you behave in such a fashion! You know Madame Chantal has been unwell. Could you not make allowances for that?'

'Madame Chantal!' Lady Lazenby gave a short harsh laugh. 'By the time I've finished spreading the word, she'll be glad to hide behind her real name — won't you, Doris Higgins?'

Madame spoke up then, her voice unusually strong. 'I'm not ashamed of my origins. At least I don't hide behind my husband's title. Everyone knows you're no lady — Isabelle Rowbottom.'

Lady Isabelle marched toward the door and Sally followed her, holding it open. As she left, she hissed in Sally's face. 'As for you, just leave my cousin alone. He has no time for the likes of you.'

Sally did not reply and with great forbearance, closed the door quietly behind her. She locked it and went over to where Madame slumped in her chair, her face ashen.

'Oh, Sally, what have we done?' Madame said. 'She'll make trouble for sure. I shall be ruined.'

'I'm sorry. I should have tried to smooth things over instead of speaking to her like that.' But Sally wasn't sorry — only on Madame's account. The business had suffered enough already without losing their clients due to rudeness and incompetence.

'I don't blame you for throwing her out. I wish I had done it. But I was so shocked. She just flew in here like a whirlwind and started raving.' Madame still looked exhausted, but the colour was beginning to return to her face.

'I knew she had a temper, but I've never seen anyone carry on like that — especially a Lady,' Sally said.

'Like I said — she's no lady. How she managed to catch a Lord I'll never know. I wonder how long it took him to realise what he'd let himself in for.' Madame gave a weak chuckle. 'It was almost worth losing a customer to see the way you dealt with her.' She leaned back in her chair and looked round at the devastation.

'I'll get Jenny to clear this up,' Sally said hastily.

'No, I'll do it later. Send Jenny home. You and I need a little talk.'

When Jenny had gone, Sally locked the door and followed Madame slowly upstairs to her attic room. She sat at the little table by the window, biting her lip, convinced that she was about to be dismissed.

Before Madame could speak she tried to apologise again, but her employer held up a hand to silence her. She sat down opposite Sally and folded her hands on the table in front of her.

'I have come to a decision,' she said.

Here it comes, Sally thought, holding her breath.

'Things have been very difficult these past few months. I have never felt really well since that bout of flu and now . . . ' Madame passed a hand over her eyes. 'As you know, my sight has been failing. I did not want to admit it but lately . . . well, I can no longer deny it. This last fiasco had proved to me that I have been deceiving myself.'

'Oh, Madame, I am so sorry.' Sally stretched out a comforting hand.

'You've been so good to mc and I have not appreciated your help, Sally. No-one else would have stood by a deluded old woman the way you have. You kept my business going, paid my debts and I rewarded you with sarcasm and cold silences. It would not surprise me if you walked away now and left me to it.' There was no trace of self pity in Madame's voice and Sally admired her self possession.

It was time for her to be honest too. 'I was not entirely disinterested, Madame. I did it for myself too. I wanted to prove that I could run a business as well as make hats to rival yours.' She took a deep breath. 'I even dreamed of starting my own business and taking away your customers.'

'But you didn't.' Madame smiled. 'You used your savings to prop me up when you could have put them to an entirely different use.'

'I could still have started up on my own you know.' Now that Sally had started she had to confess everything. 'I had an offer . . . someone was prepared to invest . . . ' She faltered and Madame smiled.

'A man, no doubt.'

Sally nodded miserably. 'But I refused.'

'Well, now it looks as if Lady Lazenby will try to ruin me so perhaps you should have taken up this man's offer.'

'Oh, no, Madame. I couldn't. I admit

I was tempted, but it wouldn't be right. He would expect something in return . . . ' Her voice trailed away and she felt herself beginning to blush. At least she could console herself that Madame had not heard Lady Lazenby's last words and had no idea who the man was.

She looked up in surprise as Madame started to laugh. 'And how do you think Doris Higgins from Bethnal Green managed to set up her own business and become a milliner to the upper classes?' She waved a hand as Sally began to speak. 'It was all a very long time ago, my dear. But as you see, I managed to survive alone all these years.'

Sally didn't know what to say, staring at her employer open-mouthed.

Madame laughed again, then grew serious. 'I was not entirely mercenary, you know. I did love him. And he . . . ' She nodded. 'Yes, I think he did love me, in his way. But he was very conventional. Unlike Lord Lazenby, who was willing to flout convention and marry his harlot.'

'If you knew about Lady Lazenby's past, why were you so keen to keep her custom? Surely you could hurt her more than she could hurt you?'

'Oh, she's a sly one. She likes to be seen as a leader of fashion so it suited her to patronise me and recommend me to her friends. I could have refused to deal with her, but she knew who my secret love was and threatened to expose him. Despite everything, I would not cause a scandal for him and his family. He was married and had a child. That's why I allowed her to treat me so rudely — and why I did not insist that she paid her bills.'

'And now I have ruined everything for you. Oh, Madame, if only I had known.' Sally started to cry.

'It's not your fault. If I had not been so proud and stubborn, her hat would not have been spoilt and she would have had no reason to complain.'

'But I should not have interfered.'

'It doesn't matter now, my dear.

Isabelle Rowbottom can no longer hurt me. My love died long since.' She sighed. 'I don't know why I didn't have the courage to stand up to her long ago.'

'But what will we do if she carries out her threat? We need those society ladies.'

'I don't think she will. But even if she does, I think we have enough clients to carry on — people like Miss Willoughby and Mrs Bailey. I know they have no time for her Ladyship's airs and graces. They will recommend their friends, you'll see. Which brings me to my decision . . . ' Madame paused and took a breath. 'I have decided that it is time Madame Chantal went back to being plain Doris Higgins.'

'You mean to retire?' Sally asked.

'Not at all. But I would like to make you my partner — an equal partner. We could move to new premises under a new name. What do you think?'

'I don't know what to say. It's such a surprise. But it sounds like a perfect idea to me.'

'Well, I don't expect an answer straight away. We can work out the details later.' She slumped back in her chair once more. 'And now, I think it would be best if you went home. I'm quite exhausted.'

When Sally got home she went straight to the dresser and reached for the tin on the top shelf. She tipped the meagre collection of coins out on to the table and sat down to count them. Tempting as it was to accept Madame's offer of a full partnership, she still hoped deep down that it would be possible somehow to start up on her own.

She had a great regard for Madame and was grateful for all she had taught her. But she had a feeling that after so many years as a mere apprentice and lately as an assistant, Madame would still look on her as an employee. She would never allow her to make decisions about the business and she would still have to seek approval of her designs.

Ada came in from the back yard as Sally was counting the money for a second time, sighing over the amount.

'Looking at it won't make it grow,' Ada said.

Sally laughed. 'You're right, Mum.' She swept the coins into a pile and put them back in the tin. 'Oh well, it looks as if my only hope is to accept Madame's offer.'

'What offer's that then?' Ada asked.

Sally told her what had happened at the salon.

'I already got most of it from Jenny,' Ada said, laughing. 'I know it isn't really funny, but I'd love to have seen the look on Lady Lazenby's face when you showed her the door.'

'I have to admit, I can see the funny side now, though I was quaking in my boots at the time, thinking Madame would give me the sack.'

Ada sat down suddenly, putting a hand to her chest. 'Oh, I'm sorry, love. She didn't, did she? Is that why you were counting your savings?'

'No, quite the opposite. She's offered to make me a partner.'

'That's wonderful.' Ada put a hand on her daughter's arm. 'It is, isn't it? Oh, I know you wanted to start up on your own, but this is the next best thing. You practically ran that salon when Madame was ill and you say she's almost blind now so you would be in charge.' She stood up. 'I'm so proud of you, love. You deserve something after all you've done for her.'

Sally didn't reply and Ada looked at her in concern. 'What's wrong, love?'

As Sally burst into tears, she put her arms round her daughter, patting her back and murmuring. 'Come on, love it can't be that bad. Tell me . . . '

Her sympathy made Sally cry all the harder, but after a few minutes she sniffed and wiped her eyes. 'Oh, Mum, I had such hopes and dreams,' she said. 'But you're right — this is the next best thing. I should be happy that Madame thinks so much of me.'

She hesitated then explained her

misgivings. 'If we're going to be partners I would want an equal say and I have lots of ideas for improving the way we work. But she's such a stubborn old thing and she's been the boss for so long . . . ' Her voice trailed away.

'I think you're being silly, love. You said yourself she's almost blind and she's not in the best of health. I think she sees this as a way to carry on a bit longer.' Ada stared at her intently. 'That's not what made you cry, though is it?' she asked.

Sally decided to tell her mother everything. 'I could have my own salon if I wanted,' she said and proceeded to confess the interest Charles Carey had shown in her.

'Oh, Sally, how could you even consider . . . '

'I didn't, Mum — not really. It just seemed . . . ' Her voice trailed away again, then she spoke more strongly. 'I refused, Mum. I told him it wouldn't be right. Besides, it's not Charles Carey I was crying over.'

'It's that footman at the Lazenbys', isn't it — Harry Jenkins.' Ada flapped a hand and laughed at Sally's astonished expression. 'There's not much goes on in this family escapes my notice.'

'But he doesn't even like me, and he said such horrible things last time we met. He thinks I'm . . . ' Sally couldn't say the words although she did manage not to start crying again. Instead she sat up straight and blew her nose. 'I never thought a man would reduce me to tears. I always swore I'd never get caught up in all that.'

Ada smiled. 'There's nothing you can do about it when you meet the right one. I remember the first time I saw your dad.' A wistful smile lit up her careworn face. 'We were always hard-up and life was a struggle, especially when you kids came along. But we had some good times. We were happy for a while, until . . . '

Until the accident that left Ada a widow with no money and a family to support, Sally thought, squeezing her mother's hand. Watching her mother struggling to bring them up had been at the root of her own wish for financial success and independence.

Her selfish ambition had made her forget the good times. The sadness in her mother's eyes now reminded her that she was luckier than most in her position, even if the man she loved did not feel the same way about her.

When Sally arrived at the salon the next day she was carrying the battered biscuit tin. Her decision was made and the money was to be her contribution to the partnership.

It was obvious Madame's health was deteriorating and although she did not wish her employer ill, there would come a time when Madame would have to leave decision making to her.

Her talk with her mother the previous evening had forced her to acknowledge her feelings for Harry and she knew that if there was a chance he returned those feelings she would give up her ambitions in a blink.

Today she firmly pushed Harry Jenkins out of her mind and greeted Madame Chantal with a smile. 'Did you really mean what you said yesterday?' she asked.

'Of course. Have you decided?' Madame hesitated. 'I would quite understand if you refused. After all, as you well know, business has not been so good lately.'

'But it will pick up, Madame, I know it will.'

'I wish I had your confidence, Sally. I'm not sure if it might not be better to retire gracefully, to leave you free to find yourself a situation where they can appreciate your talent.' When Sally started to protest, she held up a hand to silence her. 'I'm old and tired and worn out. The burden of running the business would fall on you, my dear. Are you sure that's what you want?'

Sally's heart leapt. It was exactly what she wanted. But she tried to hide her elation. 'I'm sure I can manage — with you to teach me. I've learned so much from you already, Madame.' She put the tin on the table and opened it. 'I'd like to invest this in the partnership,' she said.

'But you've given so much already. I regard the money you used while I was ill as your investment. That way we start with a clean slate and no obligations on either side — equal partners.'

'I'll only consider us equal if you accept this as well.'

'Very well.' Madame put out her hand and Sally shook it. 'Now, to work,' she said, pushing back her chair. 'We can sort out the details later, but we have a client due any minute and this place needs tidying up.'

10

To Sally's surprise, the partnership was working out far better than she'd expected, although they still sometimes disagreed about how things should be done. Sally still felt they should turn the salon into a shop, with eye-catching displays to tempt passers-by. But Madame would not give up the idea that it was better to have a few regular clients and to rely on word of mouth for recommendations. But as Sally pointed out, it only took one like Lady Lazenby to withdraw her custom and others followed. Add to that the notorious propensity of the gentry to ignore their bills and it wouldn't be long before the business started to falter again.

'But her Ladyship is only one among many and we've already proved we don't need her any more,' Madame said. 'Besides, I don't think there was anything wrong with that hat we made her. She was just out to make trouble.'

Sally bit her lip. Madame had conveniently forgotten that it was the poor workmanship caused by her failing sight that had sparked off Lady Lazenby's temper. But she couldn't say anything.

Still, things were picking up nicely since Miss Willoughby had recommended so many of her friends. And maybe the move to new premises with a new salon name would force Madame to see the advantages of changing their methods.

Every spare moment was spent traipsing round inspecting empty shops. It had to be in a good area yet with an affordable rent and it was proving hard to find the right place. These days Sally was too busy to think about romance, or the lack of it, in her life.

It was only when she was trying to get some sleep at night that thoughts of the handsome footman stole into her heart. She had not seen Harry since that disastrous encounter in the park. It hurt that he thought badly of her and she longed for the chance to put things right.

On her walks in the park on a Sunday, she scarcely listened to Rose's excited plans for her wedding as she scanned the crowds for a sight of the man she loved.

One gloomy November afternoon she had persuaded Rose to come out for a stroll, even though a thin cold drizzle had started. She couldn't bear to stay indoors if there was the remotest chance of seeing Harry.

As the rain started to fall harder, Rose pulled at her arm. 'Let's go, I'm cold,' she complained.

Sally shrugged and agreed. There was no point in hanging around in the cold. As they walked towards the park gate, she caught a glimpse of a blond head and she started forward eagerly. 'It's Harry, I must talk to him,' she said, pulling Rose with her.

Rose waved, trying to catch his eye,

but Sally stopped suddenly. 'He's with Maggie,' she gasped. 'I thought you said . . . '

'That's what he told me. They're just friends,' Rose said.

'Oh, yes — they look very friendly,' Sally scoffed. Maggie was hanging on Harry's arm and smiling up into his face. He was laughing at something she said.

Sally turned away.

'Aren't you at least going to say hello?' Rose asked.

Sally didn't reply. She just walked briskly away in the opposite direction, scarcely noticing that Rose hadn't followed. When she reached the other gate at the opposite side of the park, she looked back to see the three of them still in conversation.

Pretending she did not care, she hurried home and ignoring her mother's shocked exclamation at her wet clothes, rushed upstairs and shut herself in her room. She did not come down, even when Ada shouted up that tea was ready and when Jenny came to bed, she pulled the blanket over her head and pretended to be asleep.

When she woke next morning she felt ashamed of the way she had rushed off and left Rose standing in the rain. She would have to pop round after work to apologise.

But when Madame greeted her at the salon waving a piece of paper, she knew there would be no time to call on Rose that evening.

'I think we've found it, Sally,' Madame said, her face creased in a smile. This is just what we've been looking for.' She spread the advertisement on the desk, pointing out the features of the shop. 'Three large rooms on the ground floor and living accommodation above.' She lowered her voice. 'It's even got indoor facilities — on both floors.'

Sally smiled. The only toilet here was outside in the tiny backyard and it had caused immense problems when Madame had been ill and unable to manage the stairs. She read through the specifications again. Madame was right — it was perfect. 'But surely the rent will be too much?' she said.

'We'll go and find out, as soon as we've dealt with today's clients. I've arranged to meet the agent,' Madame said folding the paper and tucking it into her bag.

Sally thought the day would never end, but at last the workroom was tidied and the last client shown the door. She sent Jenny home with a message for her mother that she would be late and waited impatiently for Madame to get ready.

The new premises were several streets away, but still within walking distance of Sally's home. Although not in the fashionable part of the West End where the large stores vied for custom, the building was well situated for passing trade and surrounded by other genteel trades — a boot maker, a gentlemen's outfitter and a haberdasher. Sally's spirits rose. Surely here

Madame would see the benefits of changing her business practices.

From the outside, the building more than lived up to her expectations, its bow-fronted windows flanking a flaking front door with steps and a wrought iron hand rail leading up to it.

Sally could see past the peeling paint and rusty railing, pictured as it could be with a little hard work. 'It's perfect,' she said, eyes shining.

'You haven't seen the inside yet,' Madame warned. 'It may need too much work doing. Besides, the rent is bound to be too much for a building this size.'

The agent was waiting for them and he ushered them inside, anxious to point out the more desirable features in the dilapidated premises. The front door opened directly into a large salon and the sun streaming through the bow window lit up the dusty panelled walls and the rough wooden floor.

'As you can see, a well-proportioned room with original panelling,' he said, waving an expansive hand.

When Madame looked doubtful, Sally hastily intervened. 'It needs a good scrub and some polish, that's all,' she said. Her imagination was working overtime and already she could see the furniture from the old salon arranged here — Madame's desk where she could write the orders, comfortable chairs and low tables arranged so that their clients could relax, sipping their refreshments as they waited for their fittings.

A smaller room to the other side could take the full length mirror and dressing table where clients could try on their new hats. And through an arched door at the rear was another large room which would make an excellent workroom.

There was also a stockroom with plenty of storage space for bolts of cloth and cumbersome hat boxes — so much better than the cramped walk-in cupboard at the present location. Best of all was the natural light which streamed in through the large windows.

They went upstairs, Sally exclaiming in delight at the neat little kitchen with its sink and cooking range, the pretty sitting room with windows looking on to the street and a small bedroom.

Madame pursed her lips and shook her head. Sally wondered what was wrong. But they would both have to agree and she hoped she could overcome any objections Madame had.

There was still the question of the rent though. Sally held her breath as Madame asked the crucial question. The sum the agent named made them both gasp and Sally's stomach lurched as she tried to swallow her disappointment.

But Madame smiled grimly. 'You didn't strike me as the sort of man to take advantage of a poor old woman,' she said. 'Anyone can see this place needs a lot of money spending on it. It's only worth half that.' She took Sally's arm. 'Come along, we have other places to view before it gets dark.'

Before Sally could protest they were outside on the pavement. The agent hurried after them. 'My dear Madame, I assure you I had no wish to take advantage. It *is* a very desirable premises, despite the somewhat dilapidated appearance . . . '

'But the rent is too high. Come Sally.'

'Perhaps we can come to some arrangement. The owner is most anxious for the place to be occupied. He left it to my discretion . . . '

Madame appeared to consider and Sally had to hide a smile as it dawned on her what her friend was up to and why she had shown no enthusiasm as they were shown round. She was glad now that she had not tried to interfere and her patience was rewarded when the agent named a sum that was well within their means.

After a few moments when she appeared to be considering the offer, Madame held out hand. 'Agreed,' she said. 'We'll call at your office tomorrow to sign the papers?'

A time was settled and the agent hurried away, leaving the two women chuckling. 'Didn't he squirm?' Sally said. 'You certainly got the measure of him all right. I am sure he was intent on taking his share on top of his agent's fee if we had agreed to his original sum.'

'Years of dealing with haughty society ladies has taught me a lot,' Madame replied. As they walked away she became more thoughtful. 'I hope we have done the right thing. There is a lot to be done and I fear I shall be little help.'

'We have Jenny, who is quite strong for her age and a tireless worker,' Sally reassured her. 'And I am sure one of my brothers would lend a hand if necessary.'

Getting the salon ready involved far more than they'd anticipated. As well as soap and scrubbing brushes, the rooms needed several coats of paint, but their hard work was rewarded when at last it was complete.

The floorboards had been waxed to a

glistening honey colour to match the waist high panelling, the wall above painted white to reflect as much light as possible and also to show off the framed sketches of her hat designs.

A framed full-length mirror had been hung on the back of the dressing-room door which reflected light and allowed clients to see the full effects of their new millinery.

At last they were ready for the grand opening of *Maison Chapeau* as the new venture was to be called. With the new name, Madame had abandoned her pretensions to French antecedents and now insisted that Sally call her Doris, although she still felt a French name added a little tone to the business.

After a lot persuasion, she had finally agreed they should make the most of the bow windows and Sally's brother, George, who was a carpenter, had installed wide shelves covered in rich deep blue velvet across the embrasures.

Two splendid hats had been made for the occasion and now rested on display stands in the windows, surrounded by a tastefully arranged selection of gloves, scarves and jewellery. When Madame — Doris — walked outside to view the display, she exclaimed with pleasure and her objections that the salon would look too much like a shop were finally overcome.

Jenny had been allowed to take a day off school to help with the opening celebrations and now stood behind a long table, covered with a white sheet in lieu of a tablecloth, on which was a selection of delicate cakes and pastries made by Sally's mother. The whole Williams family had become involved in the project and Sally hoped that Madame would not feel too over-whelmed. But she seemed to be enjoying the occasion and was showing more animation than she had for months.

It was hard to believe she was the same frail old woman who had been almost at death's door less than a year ago.

Sally watched her once more checking the guest list and smoothing down the new russet coloured gown she had bought for the occasion, a smile of eager anticipation on her lips.

They had invited their most prestigious clients to the opening, hoping that they would at the same time obtain some orders. Sally had also persuaded her partner to insert an advertisement in *The Lady*, a magazine enjoyed by society and the middle classes which should bring in more custom.

As the clock struck, she hurried to open the door, praying that sufficient people would turn up to make their efforts worthwhile. There were several carriages drawn up in the street and a group of ladies walking towards the salon, many with maids in attendance. Sally smiled a welcome and held the door open for their guests, glancing across the street to where another carriage had just come to a halt.

Her heart skipped a beat as she saw Harry Jenkins appear from behind it.

Lady Isabelle had not been invited today so what he was doing here, she wondered? The street, despite being a busy commercial road, did not house the kind of business that a footman would frequent.

She turned away hastily, hoping he had not seen her, as she firmly tried to still the trembling in her limbs and concentrate on giving the best impression to their potential clients.

But as she smiled politely, offering refreshments and showing samples of her designs to the ladies, her thoughts were with the young man who had stolen her heart. Why was it that just a brief glimpse of him could shake her so?

She should be thrilled that at last she had achieved her dream but, looking round the glittering assembly, the fruits of her labours over the past few weeks, she realised that it meant nothing if she had no one to share it with.

11

It was almost spring again, a time when ladies' thoughts turned to new hats in pastel colours adorned with flowers and chiffon and plumes of dyed feathers — the kind of millinery Sally loved to create. She was in her element as new orders flooded in. Doris, too, seemed much happier and healthier since the move. The spacious premises with their abundance of natural light made work much easier for both of them.

The new venture was proving to be a success, so much so that they had taken Sally's sister on as an apprentice. Jenny was eager to learn and although she did not have the creative flare of her older sister, she was a neat and competent worker.

As Sally had hoped, her eye-catching window displays were bringing some passing trade and although Doris was worried that her reputation for exclusive millinery for the gentry might suffer, she had been forced to agree that the resulting extra work that came their way was worth it.

Their fortunes were certainly on the up and Sally told herself she couldn't be happier. She'd got what she wanted and whenever the image of a certain golden-haired young man with a cheeky grin stole into her thoughts, she pushed it firmly away.

She did not need a man to make her happy. She had her independence, fulfilling work that nurtured her creativity and best of all, she was able to ease the financial burden on her family. What more could she ask for?

Of course, it would have been easier to forget Harry if she never saw him. But just lately he seemed to pop up everywhere she looked. When she'd seen him passing on the day the salon opened it could have been a coincidence. She could have even imagined it since he was in her thoughts so often.

But it wasn't her imagination or coincidence that almost every time she looked up from her work, or opened the salon door to show a client out, he seemed to be walking past on the other side of the road.

Once or twice she had raised a tentative hand in greeting, but he hadn't seemed to notice her, just strode past, eyes focused ahead of him, shoulders squared, his step purposeful. Where was he going? And how did he manage to get so much free time from his job?

If he were on an errand for his Lordship, surely he would be wearing his smart footman's livery?

It was a mystery that had played on Sally's mind more than she would have believed possible only a few months ago, when the height of her ambition had been to run her own business.

And it would only be solved if she could summon up the nerve to accost him and ask him outright what he was up to.

'Well, why don't you then?' Rose asked when Sally confided in her friend. They were sitting at the kitchen table in Tanner's Lane going over the arrangements for Rose's wedding. Thomas had got leave at last and they were to be wed at Easter.

'I can't, can I?' Sally wailed. 'He'll know I'm interested in him.'

'Well, you are, aren't you?' Rose said matter-of-factly. 'And he's interested in you — why else would he spend so much time round your way?'

'But why doesn't he speak to me? No, there must be some other reason.' Sally's shoulders slumped.

'One of you has to make the first move,' Rose said firmly, standing up and announcing that it was time she went home.

She was right, Sally thought as she got ready for bed that night. I'll swallow my pride and ask him what he's up to the very next time he passes the salon.

But the next time she saw Harry she was busy with a client and by the time she had finished, he had reached the end of the road. She stood at the front door for a moment, enjoying the weak spring sunshine and biting the edge of her nail in frustration. She looked back into the salon. Jenny was tidying the fitting room and Doris was at her desk writing in her ledger.

'Do you mind if I pop out for a few minutes, Madame,' Sally asked. She still found it hard to call her old employer by her Christian name. 'There are no appointments booked for the next half-hour.'

'Of course not, Sally. You don't need to ask.' Doris scarcely looked up from the column of figures she was adding up.

Sally went down the steps, trying to appear casual and started in the direction Harry had been walking. By now he had disappeared and she paused, wondering if she was doing the right thing. But she had to find out what he was up to.

She turned the corner and saw him

going through an archway. *Carver and Jenkins, Coachbuilders,* it said.

Harry must have changed his job, but surely he hadn't gone into business for himself? And why not, she thought, she had done it and he had told her of his ambitions. She frowned. She was sure he'd wanted to work with those new-fangled horseless carriages. So he hadn't quite achieved his dream then.

Just then a loud noise burst from the building which Harry had entered, accompanied by a smell of smoke and something she could not identify. What was he up to? There was only one way to find out. But as she took a hesitant step forward, a figure came rushing round the corner and almost knocked her over.

A hand reached out to steady her and a voice she knew well began to apologise. She pulled away when she recognised Charles Carey and ran back round the corner towards the salon. It would be just her luck for Harry to see them together.

But Charles followed her, grasping her wrist and stepping in front of her. He looked her up and down, his mocking gaze taking in the new gown and smartly buttoned boots she was wearing and she wondered how she had ever even fleetingly felt the slightest attraction to him.

He glanced over her shoulder at the smart frontage of the salon with its elegant window display. *'Maison Chapeau,'* he murmured. 'My goodness, you have done well for yourself — and without my help.' He chuckled, tapping his cane against his chin and smiling insolently. 'But I hardly think this little enterprise has been achieved by your own efforts. Now who is the lucky man, I wonder?'

'How dare you insinuate . . . ?' Sally was incoherent with rage. The cheek of the man.

He laughed, still gripping her wrist. 'Come, come, Sally. I think you protest too much. I know full well you were seriously considering accepting my offer to invest in your own enterprise. And you could not have managed all this in such a short time on your own. You must have had a better offer. So who is he?'

The malicious gleam in his eyes brought a surge of rage. The new button boots had pointed toes and the kick Sally aimed at his shin caused him to yelp in surprise and fury. But he did not let go of her.

'You little wildcat. It's time you were taught a lesson,' he panted, raising his cane above his head.

Sally tried to kick him again. 'Let me go,' she screamed.

'Yes, let the lady go,' a quiet voice from behind him said.

Charles turned, arm still raised, his anger turning to laughter as he saw who it was. 'Lady?' he sneered. 'I see no lady here.'

'And you are no gentleman, sir.' Harry's voice was quiet but insistent. 'Let her go, I said.'

Charles' arm dropped to his side and

he gave a nervous laugh. As he stepped away from her, Sally aimed another kick at his shins. He leapt back with a little yelp and she could not help laughing as, no longer the smooth, sophisticated man about town, he straightened his cravat, settled his hat more firmly and scuttled away round the corner.

Sally rubbed her wrist and smiled ruefully. Now was her chance to clear the air between them. But all she could say was, 'Thank you. I'm glad you showed up.'

Harry did not return the smile. 'Glad to have been of service,' he said raising his hat and walking quickly away.

She took a step after him then stopped, despair and anger warring in her heart. Would all their meetings end like this — he believing the worst of her, she unable to find the words to tell him how she felt? Anger won and she marched smartly back up the street. Let him think what he liked. She knew the truth.

As she neared the salon, the beautifully painted sign over the shop door and the artistic arrangements in the bow windows brought a lift to her spirits. But best of all was the sight of the fashionably dressed ladies coming and going through the newly-painted door.

As she had so many times before, she ignored the pain in her heart and concentrated on her achievements. It was what she had always dreamed of after all.

12

'Keep still, Rose. How can I fix this if you keep fidgeting?' Sally's voice was muffled by the hat pin she had in her mouth.

Rose giggled. 'I can't help it. I'm so excited.'

Sally thrust the pearly-headed pin through the tiny bonnet that held her friend's veil in place and stepped back to admire the effect. Since she and Madame — *Doris* as she had at last learned to call her — had opened the salon, Sally had not much time for her friend. But she had kept her promise to design and make the wedding finery, devoting every spare minute to the hats and dresses, as well as the posies of artificial flowers that the bride and her attendants would carry.

The long dress had a row of tiny pearl-coloured rosebuds sewn down the front and around them and the little lace cap was covered in the same flowers. It had taken her hours to make each individual bud and as she swung Rose round to face the full-length mirror she couldn't help feeling pleased and proud of the results. 'You look lovely,' she said, her eyes shining with happiness for her friend.

'So do you,' Rose grinned. 'It'll be your turn next.'

'I don't think so.' Sally had told her friend about the latest encounter with the two men in her life. 'I haven't had a chance to see Harry and try to explain — not that it would help. He seems to want to believe the worst of me.'

'That's not true. I'm sure that the next time you meet, he'll have a very different attitude.' Rose was smiling secretively.

But before Sally could question her, Mrs Parker called up the stairs. 'Come along, you two. You must be ready by now.'

With a final tweak of the veil, Sally

pushed her friend out of the room. They paused at the head of the stairs, smiling at the gasps of admiration from Mr and Mrs Parker. Even Colin, Rose's little brother, looked suitably impressed. 'You look like a princess,' he said.

As they reached the hall, Mr Parker held out his arms and gave his daughter a hug.

Sally opened the front door and looked down the road to see if the car had arrived — a motor car with a special driver — chauffeur they called it. No expense had been spared for Rose's special day. The vehicle came round the corner with a chugging grinding sound and pulled to a halt in front of the house.

Hordes of small children, and some grown-ups, rushed forward to take a closer look at this strange vehicle, the like of which had never been seen in the street before. The open-topped vehicle looked like a normal carriage, but without the horses. It was painted a rich chestnut brown with shiny brass fittings that gleamed in the sunshine. There was a seat at the front for the driver and two higher seats behind it, all upholstered in tan leather.

The church was only a couple of streets away, but Mr Parker had decreed that his only daughter should arrive in style at her wedding. Sally, Colin, Mrs Parker and Daisy, the small cousin who was the only other bridesmaid, were to walk.

As they reached the street corner, Sally turned to smile and wave at her friend, surprised to feel a slight pang of envy. Mr Parker was helping her up the step into the motor car while the chauffeur held the door open. He leaned forward to settle the bride in her seat, making sure the long skirt did not get caught in the door.

Before he could replace the hat Sally caught a glimpse of a shock of gold hair and her heart gave a little lurch. 'Harry,' she breathed. But it couldn't be. Her imagination was playing tricks again. It was because he was in her thoughts, especially today, that she had thought it was him.

'Come along, Sally. We want to get to the church before the bride,' Mrs Parker called, hurrying the two children along.

And with an effort, Sally pulled herself together and caught up with them. At the church, where a small knot of well-wishers and sight-seers had gathered on the pavement, she handed Mrs Parker and Colin into the care of one of the ushers.

Everything was going smoothly, but she thought the gasps were more for the unusual sight of a motor car than for the bride herself. She forced herself to go to the church door to greet them, but as the chauffeur leapt from his seat and opened the car door, she shrank back into the shadows of the porch. It *was* Harry.

What on earth was he doing here? She knew he'd changed his job, not that he was working with motor cars. It explained Rose's smirk earlier, but why hadn't she mentioned that he was driving her to the church.

There was no time to ask her as the organ swelled and Mr Parker held out his arm, a proud smile on his face. Rose laid her hand on his arm, her face radiant, the very picture of a blushing bride.

Sally took Daisy's hand and fell into step behind her friend. As they started their stately progress down the aisle, Rose turned round and gave her a most unbride-like wink.

The ceremony passed in a blur and it seemed only moments before Sally found herself following the newly-weds into the vestry. She pulled herself together to witness her friend's signature in the register. And then they were all proceeding back up the aisle, the music reaching a crescendo as the party reached the porch and came out into the bright sunshine of a spring day.

The motor car was waiting, the chauffeur standing smartly at attention beside the open door. Sally steeled herself to look at him, but he refused to meet her eye.

A photographer appeared and they all stood to attention, holding their breath as he dived under his black cloth and told them all to 'smile please.' Sally's face already felt stiff from trying to keep a smile on her face. Then Rose and Thomas were climbing up into the motor car for the short drive back to the Parkers' house where refreshments had been laid on for friends and family.

By the time Sally arrived with Daisy and Colin, the motor car was parked outside in the narrow street, already swarming with small boys asking excited questions of Harry. Small wonder that he did not notice her as he strove to keep their grubby hands off the shiny brass and polished coach-work.

Colin hung back to gape at the wondrous machine, but Sally scarcely paused and followed Daisy into the crowded front room where a neighbour was passing round plates of ham sandwiches and sausage rolls.

Rose was in the centre of the crowd, her face flushed and excited as she clung to Thomas's arm. The beer and sherry flowed, toasts were drunk the room got hotter and noisier. Each time the door opened, heralding yet another helper with plates of food, Sally looked up. Surely Harry would have been invited in for some refreshments? But what if he did come in? What could she say to him, that's if she could make herself heard above the hubbub?

Rose and Thomas were going down to Broadstairs for a weekend's honeymoon before moving into their married quarters at the Regimental Barracks. Was Harry still outside, waiting to drive them to the station?

At last Sally could bear it no longer. She might never have another chance to put things right between them. Maybe Rose had planned for this to happen — that's what the wink in the church had been about.

Excusing herself on the grounds that

she needed some fresh air, Sally took a deep breath and opened the front door. Harry was leaning against the car, one foot resting on the running board.

The children had disappeared, their curiosity satisfied for the moment. He smiled as she came slowly towards him.

'What took you so long? I thought I was going to have to fetch you,' he said with that disarming grin that had always had the power to do things to her stomach.

'Cheeky thing,' she said, attempting a lightness of tone she did not feel.

'Want to come for a ride?'

'No thanks.'

He looked a bit taken aback and she hurried to reassure him. 'I want to talk to you — and I don't think that noisy monstrosity is the best place to have a serious conversation,' she said.

'Better make ourselves comfortable then,' he said, opening the door and holding out a hand to help her up. After a brief hesitation she accepted and climbed into the high seat.

She breathed in the smell of polish and sun-warmed leather for a second and gave herself up to the luxury — not only of sitting in such an expensive vehicle, but of being with Harry, and for once not arguing with him.

'This is *really* posh. It's not yours though, is it?' she asked attempting a lightness of tone. It wasn't what she had intended to say, but she felt nervous now that she was so close to him.

'Actually it is mine — well, the firm's. I've set up with my uncle. He was a coachbuilder and I've persuaded him to go over to making cars. He does the bodywork and I do the engines. We've taken on a couple of apprentices too,' he said proudly.

'Ambitious, like me,' Sally said.

He just looked at her and she felt a fluttering in her stomach. She had to clear the air between them, even if it meant another row.

'I never got the chance to thank you for rescuing me that day,' she said, changing the subject.

'It looked like you were managing pretty well before I came along,' he said, laughing.

'It wasn't funny. That kick I gave him seemed to make things worse.'

'At least it showed him what you thought of him. But I can understand it would make him mad. He's used to getting his own way — like that cousin of his.'

'Well, he didn't get his own way with me,' Sally retorted.

Harry looked away, a strange expression on his face.

'You do believe me, don't you?' Sally put a hand on his arm, willing him to turn round. 'I know you thought I . . . ' Her voice trailed away.

'You can't blame me, Sally. Every time I saw you, he seemed to pop up and that time in the park . . . He had his arm round you and you looked very cosy together.'

'I was upset after seeing you and Maggie together,' Sally protested.

'But there was nothing . . . '

Sally felt the anger starting to rise again. 'Oh, you expect me to believe you, but it's a different story when . . . '

'I do believe you — really. It's just . . . Sally, I was jealous. He's good-looking, rich. Why wouldn't you be taken in by him?'

'Because I've got more sense, that's why,' Sally snapped. 'Besides, he only wanted to help me set up my own business — at least that's what he said. I believed him at first and then I realised he was just leading me on.'

'But you were tempted to accept his offer. I heard him talking to her Ladyship about it. She was furious. The sparks really flew that day.' He allowed himself a small grin at the memory and Sally found herself smiling too.

But she had to make him understand. 'Of course I was tempted. You know how ambitious I was. I was willing to do anything to get my own business. And then I just couldn't bring myself to . . . '

'Well, you've got your own salon now. Can you blame me for thinking what I did? It was only when Rose came to me about her wedding that I got the whole story.'

'You should have trusted me,' Sally said with a sob in her throat.

Harry took her hand. 'I did, deep down. I just let jealousy get in the way.'

'So did I — I was jealous of Maggie.'

Harry lifted his other hand and brushed away a tear. 'You were the only one. I fell for you the moment I saw you and I hoped you felt the same way.'

'I did,' she whispered.

'We've wasted too much time,' he said, pulling her towards him and pressing his lips to hers.

For a moment she responded eagerly. It was what she'd been longing for. But the realisation of where they were made her push him away. She managed to catch her breath enough to say, 'Not here, Harry. Someone might see.'

'I don't care if the whole world sees. I love you, Sally Williams and we have nothing to hide.' He pulled her towards him again.

She realised she didn't care either. 'I love you, too, Harry,' she said as she melted into his arms and surrendered to his kisses. She didn't know how long it was before she heard voices and laughter. The wedding party were coming out of the house.

She jumped up and hastily got out of the motor car, adjusting her hat and smoothing down her bodice. She knew she was blushing and she hoped the wedding guests were too intent on the bride and groom to notice.

Harry followed more slowly, replacing his peaked cap and holding the door open. Sally tried to avoid his eyes but he grinned and whispered, 'I'll be back as soon as I've dropped them at the station. Then we can carry on where we left off.'

She blushed even more, but she couldn't help laughing at his cheek.

Thomas helped Rose up into the high seat and climbed up after her. Harry closed the door and went to the front of the vehicle to crank the starting handle. As it caught in a cloud of smoke and noise, Rose stood up, careless of the vibrations emanating from the engine.

'My bouquet,' she cried, clutching the back of the seat. 'I must throw my bouquet. Catch.' She tossed it over her shoulder and Sally without thinking reached out and caught it. There were shouts of laughter as Mrs Parker said, 'Maybe there'll be another wedding soon.'

Harry paused before climbing into the driving seat. 'I hope there will be — if she'll have me.'

The crowd went back into the house to continue the party, leaving Sally standing on the pavement in a daze. It wasn't the sort of proposal she had always dreamt of and there would still be problems to overcome. She was determined to carry on the millinery business now that it was becoming a success. She couldn't give it up now. But she couldn't give Harry up either.

If there was a way to combine

marriage and career she'd find it. Hadn't she already proved that with a little determination — and a little help from your friends — dreams could come true?

THE END

We do hope that you have enjoyed reading this large print book.

Did you know that all of our titles are available for purchase?

We publish a wide range of high quality large print books including:
Romances, Mysteries, Classics
General Fiction
Non Fiction and Westerns

Special interest titles available in large print are:
The Little Oxford Dictionary
Music Book, Song Book
Hymn Book, Service Book

Also available from us courtesy of Oxford University Press:
Young Readers' Dictionary
(large print edition)
Young Readers' Thesaurus
(large print edition)

For further information or a free brochure, please contact us at:
Ulverscroft Large Print Books Ltd.,
The Green, Bradgate Road, Anstey,
Leicester, LE7 7FU, England.
Tel: (00 44) **0116 236 4325**
Fax: (00 44) **0116 234 0205**

FOREVER IN MY HEART

Joyce Johnson

With the support of a loving family, Julie Haywood is coping well with the trauma of divorce and the difficulties of single parenthood. Well on track with her medical career, she is looking forward to an exciting new promotion — not realising it will bring her into contact with Rob, a part of her past she has tried to forget. Then, when ex-husband Geoff turns up, Julie finds she has some hard decisions to make . . .

THE SKELTON GIRL

Gillian Kaye

1812: These are tempestuous times in the wool mills of the Pennine moors. Randolf Staines is introducing new machinery to Keld Mill, which will put many of the villagers out of work. Diana Skelton, whose father used to own Keld Mill, takes a strong dislike to Randolf, and when there is trouble amongst the dismissed croppers she becomes involved. It is only after a night of violence at the mill that Diana and Randolf begin to see eye to eye . . .

A NEW LIFE FOR ROSEMARY

Anne Holman

Alone since the loss of her family in an air-raid, Rosemary — newly demobbed from the WRNS — returns to her old home. But she is shocked to find that a whole family has been temporarily housed there ... With little knowledge of children and cooking, and with housework to do, she has her hands full — especially when strange things begin happening at the bottom of her garden ... Friends help her cope, as she helps them. But will she also cope when romance calls?